Also by Jack Getze:

Who is killing Austin Carr? About to be murdered—snatched off a private fishing yacht by a six-hundred-pound giant Bluefin Tuna—a down-on-his-luck stockbroker recalls the collection of events, miscalculations, and character flaws that led to his current dire predicament: Living in a truck-mounted camper on the Jersey Shore, struggling to keep up with alimony and child-support payments that no longer reflect his shrinking income, the big-smiling, wise-cracking Austin Carr has been searching for a way out of the stock and bond business.

So when his richest client tells Austin he's dying, and the future widow—a redheaded knock-out—offers tender consolation, Austin's increasingly desperate financial situation draws him deeper and deeper into a barbed web of bad behavior and deceit.

Austin's would-be killer, whom he dubs "Mr. Blabbermouth," could be any one of several suspects, as Austin's words and deeds have attracted the wrath of many in recent weeks. The potential murderers include a wacked-out professional wrestler angry over Austin's poor investment recommendations, a jealous sales manager who Austin regularly belittles, and even Austin's greedy employer whose personality traits include a nasty, violent temper.

Or could there be another suspect Austin overlooked entirely until he stepped on board that private yacht?

BIG MONEY

For Ellen
Lots of love

JACK GETZE

Jack Getze

HILLIARD HARRIS

HILLIARD HARRIS

P.O. Box 275
Boonsboro, Maryland 21713-0275

This novel is a work of fiction. Names, characters, places and incidents either are the product of the author's imagination or are used fictitiously. Any resemblance to actual persons, living or dead, events, or locales is entirely coincidental.

First Edition-March 2008
ISBN 1-59133-239-7
978-1-59133-239-8

Book Design: S. A. Reilly
Cover Illustration © S. A. Reilly
Manufactured/Printed in the United States of America
2008

For John, Jane, and Patrick

Acknowledgements:

Thanks to Lawrence C. Sylvia M.D. (Deceased), Chairman of the Department of Pathology, Monmouth Medical Center, Long Branch, NJ, for helping me create this story's autopsy summary. Any inaccuracies, oversights, or dramatizations are mine, not Dr. Silvia's.

Thanks again to Baha Jeff for helping me keep some financial facts straight.

Thanks to author Jude Hardin of Florida who wrote the first sentence of this novel for a contest published online by J. Kingston Pierce's crime fiction blog, *The Rap Sheet*.

And extra special, lobster boy thank-yous to all my craft-building friends at Writer's Retreat Workshop and Free Expressions.

My agent, Grace Morgan, anchors any and all lists. Still love ya, Toots.

PROLOGUE

Maybe it's only a ghost.

The lady's two-story house ranks as ancient, so it's no surprise the pine floorboards creak. But do I detect a certain rhythm...as in footsteps? Hope I didn't make too much noise going through her dirty laundry.

I lean back on the blood red living-room sofa and hold my breath to listen. A grandfather clock tick-tocks in the foyer. The oil-burning basement heater pops and rumbles. And yes, there...bare or stocking feet pad quickly toward me down the hall. My heart rate ratchets up to match the hurried footfalls.

I stuff the DVD under my laptop and work hard to put on my three-o'clock-in-the-morning, full-boat Carr grin. Not exactly a simple trick. And definitely not sincere. I mean, how am I supposed to be calm and forthright when this DVD suggests last night's love interest may not be the innocent beauty I imagined?

In truth, the lady headed this way could be a killer.

Clever of me to wake her up.

I don't mention her name because...well, gentlemen do not identify their secret lovers, not even by pet handles. And seeing her march out of the murky hall into the living area's yellowish lamplight strongly suggests the need for a new nickname anyway.

I gasp. Oh, my. And oops. Oh my because she's wearing nothing but white athletic socks. And oops because she's using both hands and all ten red-nailed fingers to grasp a pump-action, single-barrel shotgun.

"You found the DVD, didn't you?"Ms. Shotgun says.

"DVD?"If it wasn't for rhyming consonants, I'd be pretty much speechless. My gaze is tightly focused on her bare breasts and that shotgun in the same close-up. Visually and emotionally, it's a lot to absorb.

Her right foot slides back, toes out. Improving her balance.

"I know you found it," she says. "Wrapped in my black beach dress."

My lips move without sound. I suppose my throat might be choked with fear, but I'd rather think I'm distracted by the long curve of Ms. Shotgun's hip, the loose weight of her breasts swinging below the carved gun stock.

Watch me get a boner.

"I just checked the bathroom," Ms. Shotgun says. "You rifled the hamper, found the black dress. So...you've got my DVD."

I try taking a deep breath. On tough stock and bond clients, this often works as a show of calm sincerity. "I swear I don't know what you're talking about."

She racks a shell into the shotgun's firing chamber.

My pledge of innocence must have lacked conviction.

I lift my iBook and offer her the DVD. My heart ticks to an even quicker time. My ego slips a notch. Time was, the full-boat Carr grin and a reasonable lie got me through bumpy spots with naked women.

My heart's really thumping now, but I probably don't have to worry anymore about that potential erection.

"Play it," she says. "We'll solve the murder together."

I slide the silver disk into my Mac and wonder if I'm really going to view what the *Branchtown Sun* calls the "MISSING HOTEL MURDER VIDEO." Like smoking, this feels very unhealthy.

The DVD's first images show a thirty-ish woman primping her hair before a gilded oval mirror. Oh, my. I recognize her all right. The happy smile fooled me.

"Don't you want to fast-forward?" Ms. Shotgun says. "Get right to the choking and burning?"

On screen, the doomed victim cracks open her hotel room door. Until tonight, I would have been surprised by what I see next: Ms. Shotgun's digital image rushes inside, pushing violently into the startled hotel guest and knocking her onto the carpet.

I turn from the laptop. "So it was you."

Ms. Shotgun raises the pump-action level with my nose.

And I thought my future looked shitty last month.

ONE

One Month Earlier...

The big thing about my pal Walter Osgood, Shore Securities' biggest producer, he's like a kid when it comes to his feelings. He just can't hide them. So when I walk into Luis's Mexican Grill, see Walter at the bar and notice his every other breath is a sigh, that he's clutching his Gray Goose like a soldier with a ticket to Iraq, I know Walter's worried about seeing me.

He's got news I'm not going to like.

Great. A fitting end to a wonderful week. I've been taking it hard in the wallet, even harder in the shorts. Ever since Monday morning's annual appointment with the New York urologist.

The name's Austin Carr, by the way. Since my Series Seven stockbroker's license is temporarily suspended, instead of Senior Financial Consultant, the slick business cards in my wallet say I'm a Special Management Adviser to Shore Securities, Inc., Members of the American Assn. of Securities Dealers. In truth, I am really just a salesman—like Walter—and I work for myself. Straight commission.

If we don't sell, we don't eat.

I slide in next to Walter at Luis's horseshoe bar and touch the slick Gucci material covering my buddy's shoulder. "What the hell's bothering you?"

Another sigh from Shore Securities' number one producer of commission dollars. A bit girlish if you ask me. Maybe I've been living in Central New Jersey too long, but I find myself fighting an urge to smack him.

A lot of us stockbrokers call ourselves investment counselors, or if we have a license to sell insurance, too, then we're financial planners. We like to wear two-thousand-dollar suits, carry leather attaché cases, and think of ourselves as professionals, like doctors, lawyers. But really we're more like car salesmen.

"You worried about the business?" I say to Walter. "We'll be okay without Mr. Vick. Carmela and I can take care of his accounts, keep the numbers coming."

Walter and I agreed to meet here after work, tune up before Mr. Vick's Friday night dockside farewell party in Atlantic Highlands. Shore's boss, Vick Bonacelli, sails with his family tomorrow for Tuscany. Only his daughter Carmela refused to go. She's staying behind to help me run Shore.

"Carmela's just like her old man," I say. "Slick on the phone."

Walter shakes his head.

I like to ruminate over the shortcomings of my profession with double margaritas and a positive setting: Luis's Mexican Grill on Broad Street in Branchtown. The decor reminds me of home, the east side of Los Angeles, and Luis, the owner-slash-bartender, is mi amigo.

"Shore's a dead puppy without Vick," Walter says. "You know it better than I do."

My jaw stiffens. "Whoa, Walter. Things aren't that bad. A couple of lousy months."

"Shore's toast," he says.

I lean forward, make him look directly at me. I need to see those expressive blue eyes. If Walter really believes Shore isn't going to survive, then I can easily guess the nature of tonight's bad news.

"You're leaving?" I say.

Walter nods.

Shit. "Today was your last day?"

He nods again, then bumps his shoulder against mine. "You know how this friggin' business is," he says. "Two minutes after I'm gone, the back office is passing out my accounts and my old best friends are telling my clients I've got AIDS and ran off with my twelve-year-old babysitter."

Luis's Mexican Grill is Friday-night packed, loud and oblivious. Walter still has his voice set on whisper.

"This way," he says, "I've got a weekend to prepare my clients for your assault."

Except for math, science, history, and geography, Walter's no dummy. Guaranteed he's been tenderizing his good clients about this

4

move for weeks.

"You're a part owner, Walter. You have a piece of Shore. Why would you throw that away after only a few bad months?"

When he shakes his head this time, not a hair moves. Walter Osgood pays a hundred bucks per styling. "Shore's lost money every month since we bought in," he says. "With Vick leaving town, this A.A.S.D. investigation, Sunny and Doppler taking a walk...the red numbers can only get worse, Austin. I'm bailing."

Sunny was a complainer and Doppler spent his days distressed over potential bad weather. They've had a pissy attitude since Mr. Vick sold me, Carmela's now-estranged husband Tom Ragsdale, and Walter half of Shore's stock.

"Are you worried about this A.A.S.D. investigation?" I say. "Is that why you're leaving?"

"No," Walter says. "I'm leaving because Jaffy Ritter Clark is handing me a check for $450,000 when I show up for work Monday. But if I were you, I'd worry what that A.A.S.D. cutie might dig up on Shore Securities' marketing practices. Remember that St. Louis bond default last year? Mr. Vick's sales contest?"

I turn Walter's shoulder, make him look at me again. "You're leaving me, Vick, and Carmela dead in the water, man. Without your numbers, we are in trouble. Can't you give it another six months?"

Walter's pale blue eyes turn cold on me. "What's going to change?"

TWO

It's bad, bad news for my kids' future Walter Osgood is leaving Shore. He's our ace, earned over $900,000 in gross commissions last year. The firm is definitely teetering without Walter. And therefore so is my dream of building a college nest egg for Beth and Ryan.

After promising Walter I'll keep my mouth shut until Monday and hugging him goodbye, I ignore the urge to self-medicate right there at Luis's. I drive instead to Mr. Vick's party in Atlantic Highlands. I owe the boss at least an appearance. And with all Mr. Vick's single cousins and nieces there drinking like fish, maybe I'll get lucky.

Yeah, it crosses my mind I'd be helping my own business interests if I tell Vick about Walter leaving, bring in the guys on Saturday to work Walter's accounts. But it's only a fleeting thought. Walter's a close friend.

I park, walk straight inside the bayside restaurant bar and bubbly flow of Bonacellis and Shore Securities employees. A disk jockey's thumping disco to an overflow dance floor. Half the dancers are women bobbing and weaving with other women. I'd like my odds of taking one to bed later if it wasn't for black storm clouds hurtling down from the north.

At the bar, I order another martini. Through long windows behind the slick wood counter, I watch lightning flashes burst over Manhattan.

Feels like the world is engineering me a tempest.

When I've sipped my glass of gin and vermouth down to transportable levels, I join the crowd of familiar faces. Another Shore broker, Bobby G., and I admire the size of Mr. Vick's family and the widespread Bonacelli characteristic of large breasts. Particularly among the women.

Someone grabs my shoulder. It's Vittorio "Mr. Vick" Bonacelli himself, sole founder of Shore Securities. Thanks to this winter's deal that brought in me, Carmela and her new-then-ex husband Ragsdale—who can keep track of the latest ins and outs—and Walter into the fold as partners, Mr. Vick's current ownership is down to forty-nine percent.

But Mr. Vick is our beloved leader. He'd be the boss if that number was two percent.

"We need to talk," he says.

Mr. Vick drags me to a quiet eddy.

"I want you to look out for Carmela while I'm gone," Vick says. "I don't want her going back to Rags."

One and a half see-throughs have tuned me up enough to tell Mr. Vick exactly how I feel. I have plenty to do without watching over his Butterface daughter.

"Isn't taking care of Carmela one of Carmela's jobs now, boss? Didn't I just write her a big check for college graduation?"

Great figure, Carmela. In fact, everything about her is great. Everything BUT HER FACE.

"You call that a big check?" Vick says.

Hey, fifty bucks was all I could afford. And I think generous considering my current financial prospects. I mean, I was back on my feet until I forked over a down payment on my damn Shore Securities stock.

"Make sure you see Carmela every day," Vick says. "She's going ahead with the divorce, but she's still nutty about him. If Rags comes back, goes ape-shit again...you see Carmela with one puffy lip, you call my friend Tony. He knows what to do."

Except when he's behind the wheel of his Jaguar, the recently married-and-quickly-separated-with-a-piece-of-Shore-Rags—my former sales manager—is a pussycat. Crazy, yes. But not the hand-to-hand combat type. We'll never see him again.

"And oh, yeah," Vick says, "I told my mother to call you she gets in any predicaments."

Now there's a problemo. "Mama Bones" Bonacelli, among other nefarious enterprises, runs a chain of free senior-citizen exercise clubs as a front for her betting operations. For entertainment, she practices voodoo and shamanism. With Mama Bones, a "predicament" could easily involve the FBI, peyote buttons, or flesh-eating zombies.

"No whining about Mama," Mr. Vick says.

I must have groaned out loud.

"You owe me big time for keeping you on a personal-services contract until your A.A.S.D. suspension is over," Mr. Vick says. "And I'm letting you finish buying shares in the business out of your end of Shore's profits so you can finally start building something for your kids."

I sigh and check the shine on my Florsheims. "You're right, Vick. I'll keep an eye on Carmela. Mama Bones, too."

"Thanks." Mr. Vick clasps my hand. I feel a wad of paper pressed against my palm, and like a slick maître d collecting his cash duke, I snag the paper from Vick's hand in one smooth motion.

Later, when I'm alone, I see Vick's handout is a torn sheet of yellow notebook paper. *Tony* and a phone number are penciled in block letters. The phone number has a 718 prefix, which tells me this Tony guy resides in Brooklyn.

Wonder should I read anything into that? Vick's emergency muscle comes from big time mob country?

Nah.

THREE

It's a mournful, no-more-Walter Monday. The late winter storm that blew in Friday became a nasty nor'easter Saturday. The black sky still howls wet pellets of ice and occasional snow flakes sixty hours later. Only our nickname for Shore's newest rookie salesman—Dominic Defino (rhymes with albino) offers our bullpen any relief from a mirthless world.

Wonder what these simultaneous callers want?

Damn Defino.

Carmela informs me "Mama Bones" Bonacelli is on line one, some kind of confrontation with the Branchtown police. Oh, boy. Line two is that tight-assed sweetie from the American Association of Securities Dealers, Ann Marie Talbot. Kind of a living Betty Boop, Ann Marie wants to update me on her regulatory audit.

I'd like to update her audit.

I flip a coin to see who gets first crack at me. The nickel hits my hand but I don't look. My eyes drift instead to the empty desk where Walter sat for seven years. I smile, remembering the time we sent phone-sex into our new sales manager's first meeting.

"Hi, Mama Bones. What's up?"

"'Allo, Austin. I needa you help."

Mr. Vick's mom, Angelina Bonacelli, has lived in Branchtown, New Jersey seventy of her seventy-eight years, but she still speaks English as if she'd heard our language for the first time last week. She does this on purpose, I've decided. Makes herself sound helpless when in truth the woman is tougher than week-old tomato pie.

I tuck the phone between my ear and shoulder, plop down in Mr. Vick's padded swivel chair overlooking the Shore Securities sales

9

floor. The guys are busy on the phones. "What's the matter, Mama Bones? One of your zombies bite a cop?"

"Uppa yours, Austin," she says. "My little Vittorio say I call you if I need help. And I need your help. I'm under the arrest."

Sounds like she needs a lawyer, not a stockbroker. "You're at the police station?"

"I'm home now, but the policeman is here to take me there. He say I cheat on the bingo game."

"Bingo game?"

"What are you, a parrot? Atta the church. You know. I go every Sunday night. The policeman say the game is fixed. That I gotta go to jail. Can you believe such a thing about Mama Bones?"

As a matter of fact...

"Austin?" It's Carmela, tugging on my sleeve. "Ms. Talbot of the A.A.S.D. said to tell you she's finished the audit and that she's leaving town. She needs to talk to you immediately. And Bobby G. says you have to speak with one of Vick's clients."

Screw Talbot, the A.A.S.D., Vick's client, and Bobby G. Bingo, huh? I'm really curious about this. The world of chance is Mama Bones' oyster, and if there's a way to cheat at bingo, she's the one to have figured it out. His mother put Vick through four years at Rutgers by playing the ponies.

"Can I talk to the policeman, Mama Bones? Maybe I can straighten this out."

"Sure, smarty pants. Is why I call. Here's your friend, Jimmy Mallory."

I should have known. Branchtown Detective James Mallory and I coached our sons at T-ball together, and last year renewed our acquaintance when I got mixed up with a bad crowd, had my stockbroker's license suspended.

"Vick's mom is not under arrest," Mallory says. "I can't make her understand. She just has to come to the station with me, answer the charges. Sign a paper, then she can go."

"What charges?"

"Like she said, fixing the bingo game. Misdemeanor fraud maybe. She just answers the charges, we investigate."

"Jim, how the hell do you cheat at bingo?"

"Arrange with the priest to draw certain numbers, split the pot with him."

Wow. I've heard Mama Bones works people over better than the Rutgers offensive line, but this manipulation truly ranks as awesome. She probably convinced the priest he was doing God's work, keeping half for the church.

"Ann Marie Talbot."

"Austin Carr returning your call, Ms. Talbot. Carmela tells me you've finished your audit."

"Yes, and I have bad news."

"You're coming again next month?"

"No reason to be rude, Mr. Carr. Frankly, it's the kind of thing you don't need right now."

Ms. Betty Boop's pretty. But her tone riles the back of my neck. Worse, the pitch of her voice grates my ass. "Why's that?"

"Our audit turned up three different instances where your clients' cash balances were used to reduce your overnight broker loan. The money was only co-mingled for a day, possibly because your bank failed to follow instructions, but it's still co-mingling."

The lights of Shore's big sales room slide to dim. I notice I'm suddenly breathing through my mouth. Co-mingling is one ugly-ass word in the securities business. If the charge sticks, and the A.A.S.D. holds one of their nasty, hero-A.A.S.D.-saves-the-world-from-crooks press conferences, Shore Securities will be called thieves by every media outlet in New Jersey. Branchtown's a long way from Wall Street, but even the *Wall Street Journal* might run a story.

"Could we discuss this in person, Ms. Talbot? I mean before you turn in that report? Co-mingling's a very serious charge."

"I'm headed back to Philadelphia tonight," she says. "I don't see that there's time."

My guts twist into a tight ball. Every night Shore deposits whatever bonds, stocks, and cash we've collected during the day into our New York clearing bank, along with very specific instructions about what goes where, i.e., our account, or individual customer accounts.

"I'm returning to Branchtown next week," she says. "You can still have input at that time."

Our bank makes occasional mistakes, putting people's money in with Shore's, mixing client funds with ours. But everything gets sorted out and corrected the next morning by phone when we see a printout of what the graveyard bank shift did to us the night before.

"If the mistakes are corrected immediately, how can you call it co-mingling?" I say. "I mean, you have to find out about a mistake before you can fix it, right?"

"I'll try to call you next week," she says.

FOUR

I'm in Mr. Vick's mahogany-paneled private office, one hand on the boss's previously locked and out-of-bounds liquor cabinet, the other on an unopened bottle of forty-year-old bourbon, when I hear Carmela scream.

I have to say, my first thought is Carmela's seen a mouse. The scream is high-pitched, sort of squeaky, and I expect there's a little smile on my face when I reach Vick's office doorway to check the scene out. But it's not a mouse chasing Carmela down the center isle of Shore's half-staffed big sales room. It's a rat—Carmela's estranged husband and Shore's ex sales manager, Tom Ragsdale. More surprising, shocking even, Rags is wielding a steak knife. My old boss and nemesis is pretty fast, too.

Probably the only way to catch him is to step on his tail.

Breaking into a run, and spotting no other available appendages, I dive for his legs. I'm not really the hero type, but Rags' small and demented brain seems completely focused on catching Carmela. Plus, I personally owe this bastard plenty. Before he turned his life over to booze, drugs, and gambling, Rags actually ran me down last year with his Jaguar.

My shoulder makes perfect contact with his knee, a classic, all-pro tackle, and we tumble together in a ball of fists and elbows, crashing against the bottom of Bobby G's desk bordering the main aisle. High school football coaches everywhere would be proud of my form.

My ears await the rush of cheers and accolades from the dwindling, late Monday afternoon sales staff as I push up onto my hands and knees. But the only sound I hear are gasps.

What? Did my pants fall down?

Nope. It's Rags, up much faster than me.

As I'm still scrambling to my feet, Rags grabs Carmela, rips a bond calculator from the top of Bobby G's desk, then wraps the machine's electric cord around her neck.

"Back off, sucker," Rags says, "or I'm going to recalculate Carmela's yield to maturity."

"Tony?"

"Yeah?"

I decided to call Brooklyn. It's what Mr. Vick told me to do, and except for lining up left-to-right-breaking putts, and maybe right-to-left ones as well, Mr. Vick's past advice has proven...well, not bad.

"My name's Austin Carr. My partner Vick Bonacelli said I should call you if his daughter's jilted husband came back and caused trouble."

"Jelly what?"

"Jilted. Carmela's husband. He's here."

"Vick's in trouble?"

This guy Tony sounds like major mental midget. Hope it's just a bad first impression. "No, his daughter Carmela's in trouble. Vick's in Italy."

"Right. Uh...what's going on...exactly?"

I shake my head at the phone, then glance at Rags. He's had Carmela inside the big glass conference room for five minutes now. The door's locked and that black electric cord still winds tight around Carmela's neck like a snake. Maybe I should have called the police instead of this Tony guy, but Rags appears very scary. Beady, drug-zapped eyes. Oily sweaty skin. I'm afraid he could be too much for local law enforcement. Besides, the boss Mr. Vick told me to call Brooklyn, not the cops.

"Hey, Carr. I'm waiting here," Tony says.

"Sorry. I was just taking a look. Right this second, Rags is holding Carmela hostage inside our conference room. He has an electrical cord wrapped around her throat. I don't know what to do."

"Did he say what he wants?" Tony says.

"A hundred grand to pay off some gambling debt. Says it's a loan against the stock in Shore he's signing over to Carmela as part of their divorce settlement. The split's not a done deal yet, so he thinks he's got leverage."

"Okay, that's good. That's very good. Tell him someone's on the way with the hundred thousand."

"You want me to tell him you're going to give him the money?"

"That's what I said, right? Now get in there, tell him what I told you. And make sure he knows he doesn't get the money if he hurts Carmela."

Tony's confidence is not catching, but it does somewhat relieve my first impression. He sounds like he knows what he's talking about. Perhaps he has experience with unwrapping cords from people's necks.

"But how can I stall him for hours while you get the money, then drive down from Brooklyn?" I say.

"This is a cell phone, sunshine. I'll be there in ten minutes. Don't worry 'bout the cash."

Handsome man, Tony Farascio. Six-foot-plus. Wide shoulders. That Mediterranean-dusky thing, onyx-black hair with a beard heavy enough to sprout five o'clock shadows at breakfast. But also with delicate features; chin, nose, and cheekbones like a movie star. George Clooney pretty.

Through the conference room glass, I watch Tony show my ex sales manager what's inside his New York Giants sports bag. I'm guessing the contents must look like a hundred grand because Rags pushes Carmela closer to the glass and reaches to unlock the solid oak door.

I hold my breath.

Tony glances over his shoulder to make sure I've emptied the office of potential witnesses, then kicks the just-unlocked door in on Rags. I hear and feel the thud of the collision. Carmela goes flying, too.

Tony is inside instantly, ripping the calculator from Rags and freeing Carmela.

By the time I rush in, the skirmish is over. Rags is moaning on the floor. Carmela's crying, but standing off in a neutral corner. Tony digs in his pocket.

"Bring my car around back," Tony says.

He tosses me his keys. My hand drops from the weight of the catch. Must be fifteen or twenty keys on this NY Giants ring.

"It's the dark blue Town Car out front," he says.

Flat on his back, Rags kicks at Tony's crotch. It's wild, and pretty much telegraphed. He misses, Rags' Gucci-shoed foot barely scraping the bigger man's thigh.

Tony raises his fist and pops Rags hard in the forehead.

"Don't hurt him," Carmela says.

Too late for that, Carmela. Your hubby's eyes are rolling back into his head as we speak. He's unconscious and probably has a concussion.

Tony nods to me. "Get my car."

"What are you going to do with him?" I say.

Tony grins. "Don't worry 'bout it. Let's just say I'm going to relocate his ass. Like one of your dangerous New Jersey black bears."

FIVE

One week later, I'm grabbing a stool at the bar of Luis's Mexican Grill, anxious to eat a couple of Chef Umberto's green-chili burritos for dinner, when the world's greatest bartender comes over and leans across the counter.

"Do you know this man?" Luis whispers. His head tilts, indicating I should look in the direction of the corner booth nearest the kitchen.

I follow Luis's gaze. Looks like...it is, Joseph "Bluefish" Pepperman. Dining with two business-types, although now that I look a tad closer, both of his friends maybe a little too athletic and solid under the suits, ties, and starched white collars. Imported muscle.

"Anybody who bets in Branchtown knows Bluefish," I say. "I've never seen him in here before, though. Have you?"

Luis shrugs. "No, he has never been here before this afternoon."

Luis wears his usual black slacks and white dress shirt with the sleeves rolled up. My friend's high forehead and aquiline nose tell of European descent, but his black penetrating eyes and high cheek bones give him a distinct Native American quality as well.

"Did Bluefish say something to you?" I ask.

"No. But his arrival encouraged several of my customers to abandon their dinner plans. I believe he has more of an interest in you, does he not?"

"What? Has he been staring at me or something?"

"As soon as you walked in," Luis says.

When I tasted how oily fillet of bluefish was at a fish fry two years ago, I figured it must be Bluefish's greasy appearance that

17

earned the local bookie his nickname. The black silk shirts. The slicked back hair. The man definitely sports a slippery quality that seems to match the oily taste of the fish.

Bluefish catches me looking. Slowly, he nods his long narrow head at me in recognition.

But Bluefish's nickname has nothing to do with oil or grease; I learned that last year from my friend at the *Newark Herald-Examiner.*

"You ever see swimmers called out of the Jersey surf by the lifeguards because of a boiling mass of fish?" my friend said.

"Last summer. Somebody said it was a school of bluefish."

"I don't know if the bluefish are in a frenzy because they're eating something smaller, or because they're being eaten by something bigger," my friend said. "I never asked because I figured it didn't matter. It's the way the school acts that got Bluefish his nickname."

"Violent, you mean?"

"Out of control."

Glad I remembered that now. And truly glad that except for the ponies once in a while, I don't gamble.

This is all doubly good because, now that I've noticed them, Branchtown's minor-league version of a New York goon squad leaves the table and strolls around the bar in my direction. Another doubly good thing: I met Bluefish once at a restaurant in Spring Lake. Mr. Vick, who was taking me and some guys to dinner after a round of golf, told us he knew Bluefish from high school.

"Hey, Carr," Bluefish says. He offers his hand.

I'm surprised he remembers my name. There were four or five of us at the dinner table that night. The guy must have taken a Dale Carnegie class. I slide off my stool and shake. "Nice to see you again, Mr. Pepperman."

He slaps my shoulder like an old drinking buddy. "Call me Bluefish."

Luis says, "It is not good for my business that you are here."

Luis leans across the dark horseshoe bar, staring at Bluefish, showing all of us that windy Halloween look in his eyes I've only seen once or twice before.

"I would like you and your friends to leave," Luis says.

Thanks, Luis. Trying to get me killed?

Bluefish's two sidekicks slide up quietly beside their bookie boss, creating a wall to screen us from most of the restaurant. Bluefish's men unbutton their Italian sports coats and show us the pistols stuffed in their belts.

Luis may have to reconsider his poor hospitality.

Across the room, a young woman leads her table in sharp laughter. The TV behind the bar is blaring spring training baseball highlights. The restaurant's familiar onion, cilantro, and simmering chili smells seem suddenly sharp and pungent. My pulse is up. What the hell is it with me and guns? Suddenly, they're a major part of my life.

"Are you leaving?" Luis says. "Or will I call the police?"

I grew up in the eastern, Mexican-American section of Los Angeles. Ever since grammar school I've admired the code of honor and fierce pride with which so many Hispanics are raised. Simply put, my favorite bartender is an hombre. You feel safe drinking at his bar, but I hope Luis doesn't think the switchblade he carries in his back pocket matches him up with those two semiautomatics I saw.

"We're happy to leave," Bluefish says. "Your food looks like runny dog shit. However, Pedro, you're coming with us. I think your big mouth has earned you a spot next to Carr in my back seat. Get your ass out from behind the bar."

Luis's face hardens into wood. "I have customers. I will not leave my place of business."

Bluefish's men aim their pistols at my head.

SIX

Bluefish's black Chevy Suburban crunches gravel in Luis's parking lot and then rolls quietly across the sidewalk into light traffic. Red dash lights cast a hellish glow on Bluefish and his doublewide driver, Max, who waited for us outside and had big trouble squeezing inside the SUV.

Max would have trouble squeezing inside a bus.

Luis and I are tucked in the Suburban's middle row behind Max and Bluefish. From the jump seat behind us, Bluefish's two pals in business suits press their semiautomatics against our necks.

"Here's the deal," Bluefish says. "Tom Ragsdale is a degenerate gambler. No one will take his action. But then your asshole boss Vick tells me he'll guarantee his son-in-law's bets. Okay, I know Vick a long time. I take his word. But a few months go by, and now this hump Ragsdale is into me for eighty-nine gees."

"Rags and Vick's daughter are getting divorced," I say.

"So?"

"Well, I'm just saying. But no matter what, why is this my problem?"

Bluefish's head turns back to the windshield. "Everybody tells me Vick's coming back at the end of the summer. Maybe he does, maybe he doesn't. In the meantime, I'm holding Vick's share of Shore as collateral, meaning you and your big mouth friend are going to do me a couple of favors."

The Suburban turns off Broad St. at Newman Springs Road and heads toward the Garden State Parkway. Every other building is a gas station or a liquor store. Guess people who work in Branchtown like to fuel up before the big ride home.

"Carr, you're going to open an account for me at Shore Securities, help manage my money."

Luis raps his window with soft knuckles, listening at the glass. He silently tests the door handle, too. It's locked. The driver Max must have switched on his override. Is my favorite bartender considering a bailout?

"Sounds painless," I say to Bluefish, "but a few months from now you'll want Shore to accept bags of cash, or stolen negotiable securities. I know how this crap works. It's why Mr. Vick never opened an account for you all the time he's known you."

Luis's hand tests the door handle again. Hope to hell he doesn't leave me in here alone. Double hell. That driver Max makes my skin creep. His head is the size of a jack-o-lantern, his back and shoulders like a rhino.

"What favor do you ask of me?" Luis says.

"Liquor distribution," Bluefish says. "I got a company in Philly wants to supply your restaurant."

"No," Luis says.

Bluefish's head drops to his chest. Very expressive, this bookie. I should introduce him to Walter. "This ain't no negotiation, asshole, you and me going back and forth. Do what you're fuckin' told or I bury both of you alive in the Pine Barrens."

He nods out the window. We're on the Parkway headed south now. Manicured lines of scrub pine, oak, and maple trees border both north and south lanes. Another fifteen or twenty miles, the forest turns shorter and wilder. Nothing but scrub pine.

"Perhaps there is a third choice," Luis says. "A contest. Myself against your driver."

Turning to us, Bluefish's eyebrows jump halfway to his receding hairline. "You want a piece of Max? That's your genius solution?" Bluefish shakes his head. "You come across as smart, too, although maybe I was fooled 'cause you don't talk much. But no, I see no benefit. I've got what I want right now."

"What if I agree to include a one-quarter interest in the restaurant itself—in addition to my liquor business?" Luis says.

Wow. My man is feeling confident. Is Luis in possession of material facts of which I am unaware? Maybe something to do with that door handle?

"Hey, I'm impressed," Bluefish says. "How about you, Carr?

You're not going along with this dumb idea, are you?"

I've never gone wrong trusting Luis yet. El Hombre. He's got a mean plan, I know it.

"Sure I'm going along," I say. "Here's my offer: Max wins, you get your new account at Shore, plus I'll agree to launder cash for you, say $100,000 a month."

Bluefish scratches his narrow chin. "You're actually making this tempting," he sighs. "Max? What do you think?"

A bus zooms by in the fast lane, a steel box loaded with senior citizens and their rolls of slot change headed for Atlantic City. Max, The Creeper, shrugs as if the Suburban went over a small bump.

"Max stomp him," Max says.

Bluefish says, "Hmm. So what's the rules, Pedro?"

"No weapons," Luis says. "The fight will continue until there is only one man still able to fight."

"Sounds like a waste of time," Bluefish says. "Max?"

The driver's huge head bounces up and down maybe an inch. My pulse ticks much higher than that. This duel is going to happen. Luis versus The Creeper. A ball of imaginary grease rolls around my stomach.

"Max stomp him quick," Max says.

Bluefish stares out the car window. "Well, why the hell not."

"If I win, you will forget about these so-called favors?" Luis says.

Bluefish shrugs. "If you win? Right. Turn off at the next exit, Max. I can't look down at a fifty-dollar bill lying on the sidewalk and not pick it up."

SEVEN

The Suburban's headlights slice through the inky air like white lasers, searching the blacktop gliding toward us. Pine and oak trees border both sides of the confined two-lane road, a thick black wall of forest. Above the treetops, a narrow strip of sky shimmers with stars.

I'm definitely getting nervous. The only thing keeping my heart rate below two-hundred per minute sits calmly beside me. Luis. Like Mr. T—the former TV star who claimed fame winning The World's Greatest Bartender title—mi amigo Luis can handle anything.

The Suburban's red-glow dash lights fire up the angled edges of The Creeper's profile. Almost inhuman, really. Cartoonish. Fiery colors. Trick imaging, yes, but I can't shake the feeling he's a monster driving me and Luis on some highway to hell.

Bluefish says, "So, Max, tell the guys here about your first job. The one you had when you were thirteen."

Bluefish thinks this is funny. He covers his mouth with his fingers. Call it a silly hunch, but I'm going out on a limb here. I predict this revelation about Creepy Max's teenage past is going to make me worry even more about Luis's future.

"Max work with circus," Creeper says. Talking about himself in the third person again, his voice is a crackling whisper. Broken glass thrown on sandpaper.

"No, tell them what you did for the circus," Bluefish says.

"Max wrestle bears."

Bluefish fakes a cough. "Notice he said 'bears,' guys. Not 'bear.'"

The Suburban swings into a private driveway. Six-foot lengths of treated logs bridge the roadside ditch where water trickles through tall grass. A battered black-squirrel mailbox stands as wooden sentry. How cute, except the critter's had his head shot off. The trees outside the SUV window are broken, gnarled, and twisted pine.

Seventy-five feet off the blacktop, the forest opens into a grassy clearing and a mulched playground for kids, with slides and jungle gym, and a parking lot big enough for a dozen cars. Three brick barbecues line one side of the parking area. Probably where Bluefish holds his company picnics. Buries his wives and girlfriends.

The Suburban rolls to a stop against the parking lot's log boundary. Luis's hand is locked onto the door handle, his gaze pinned on Creeper. Luis's body language reminds me of a house cat. Watching Max like he's a mouse.

Trouble is, I figure Creeper for more the Giant Rat of Sumatra.

Bluefish saying, "Do I even need to get out of the car, Max? I mean, how long could this take?"

I hear Max click a switch. All the Suburban's doors pop free, and Luis is outside before I smell fresh air. Wow. I saw his hand move this quickly once, when some pachuco hoisted Luis by the collar and my favorite bartender went for his switchblade. But Luis's whole body is a blur this time. Like that house cat, making his move.

Poking my head outside, I see over the SUV's roof that Luis is loose and ready beside the Suburban's flank while Max still squeezes from behind the wheel like some ugly brown gob of toothpaste.

When Luis kicks Max's door, stomping on the hinged steel like he's breaking down a locked vault, Luis times his explosion. He catches Max's pumpkin-sized noggin just as Creeper's face moves between the top of the Suburban's door and the truck's frame.

Ouch. The chunky sound of steel on Creeper's thick head—like someone dropped a stick of butter—makes me wince.

Max staggers down to one knee, blood oozing from his temple. His body weaves, then tumbles face first onto the parking lot's shredded bark. The earth shakes like somebody dropped a piano.

My heart's drumming, hard rain on a cardboard roof. The two guys in suits scramble out of the Suburban's rear seat, knocking me down, pushing past. They want Luis. One rushes around the grill, the other goes for the rear bumper. My lungs want more oxygen.

Luis stoops out of my view, then reappears like magic

24

photography back inside the Suburban, scrambling into the driver's seat. One hand extends a gun toward Bluefish's head. Luis must have taken the weapon from Max. A tear of sweat rolls down my right flank.

I see Luis's end game, at last, and jump back inside the Suburban. Same seat I had before, behind Bluefish. Damned if I don't hear the hoot-hoot-hoot of a horned owl before I slam the door. Are the spirits with us?

Luis hits the override soon as my door shuts, locking the three of us inside. Luis grins as he hands me the gun. What an hombre. "Watch carefully Bluefish's hands. If you lose sight of them, shoot."

It would be my pleasure, I think. I'm no killer, but if Bluefish has another gun on him, and I don't shoot when he goes for it, Luis and/or me could suffer serious and permanent injury.

No risk taker, however, Bluefish shows me the back of his hands, one poised by each ear. How sweet. He's wearing his missing wife's wedding band. Wonder if he's still offering a reward.

I line up the muzzle with the back of Bluefish's demented cerebellum.

The two guys in suits are hammering the windows and yanking on the doors. When that fails, they start shooting. Cracks appear on the window beside Luis's head, but the bullets don't penetrate. Wow. Bulletproof glass. I'm impressed with Bluefish's defenses, and the fact Luis must have figured this out earlier. I remember him tapping the glass with his knuckles.

Luis throttles the Suburban into a bark-spewing K-turn.

Bluefish saying, "You humps are as good as dead."

EIGHT

Plenty of parking at the Mexican Grill when Luis bounces us back into his gravel lot. With no bartender to mix drinks for over an hour, Luis's thirsty customers obviously sought refreshment elsewhere. In Branchtown, drinking loyalties have certain limits.

I'm breathing like a normal Labrador again as Luis flips off the engine. My heart-rate's taken a dive, too. Probably down to a smooth one-eighty. Don't think I was meant to aim guns at people. Or maybe it's the dead-ass blank stare Bluefish just gave me. Gives me the passing thought I might be out of my league.

Luis swings his shoulders to confront Bluefish, holds up the car keys like a prize. "You will forget about the favors?"

Good thing I've got Luis, El Hombre. Now that man's in a league of his own.

Bluefish nods, reaches for the keys. "Sure."

Don't know about Luis, but Bluefish's tone and manner do not sate me with confidence. In fact, it's impossible to even hope he's telling the truth. Or maybe I'm just the skeptical type, being a stockbroker and all.

Bluefish's fingers snatch air as Luis yanks the keys back. "I would be a fool to let you withdraw if you do not plan to keep your word."

Guess Luis agreed with my zero reading of Bluefish's Sincerity Meter. Bluefish better be careful what he says next, too. I know for a fact Luis has the stomach to kill.

"I'll keep the bargain," Bluefish says. "I'm pissed off, yeah, so maybe it don't sound right. But I'll forget about the favors, wait for Vick to get back."

He tried that time. I have hope he might live up to his word. No confidence. Just hope. And actually, "forgetting about the favors" isn't exactly "I won't have someone shoot you in the head" either.

Luis gives him the keys to the Suburban.

Inside Luis's Mexican Grill, my favorite bartender has drinks to make. Not everybody's gone home. I cover a stool at the empty horseshoe bar, right under Luis's collection of authentic caballista sombreros, order one of Umberto's green chili burritos, sides of rice and beans, and a Dos Equis to wash it all down.

An hour later Umberto's gone home and the last two customers, a middle-aged couple, are sipping coffee. Luis flips off the TV and begins to toss trash, wipe glasses, and towel the counter. When the bar's clean and ready for tomorrow's setup, Luis finds two shot glasses and pours us Herradura Gold. A nightcap of warriors. Actually, I guess I was more of a foil. Or maybe a prop. Poncho to Luis's Cisco Kid.

We salute and drink.

"So, Luis."

"Si."

"I'm starting to wonder if I was really meant to be a stockbroker."

He grunts. "After tonight, it is not unreasonable to have suspicions."

Luis makes a joke. Unbelievable. "I'm serious. I need to provide for my children, and right now this is where I can make the most money, have the best chance of scoring enough for their education. But is hawking stocks and bonds really what I was born to do? My life's purpose?"

Luis pulls our glasses off the bar. Guess it's just one nightcap tonight. "Only you can answer such a question. But I agree that a man should have purpose."

"I have an old friend who's a fireman," I say. "Doesn't get paid much, and he's always arriving at the scene before the ambulance, trying to save or resuscitate the most horribly mangled accident victims. But he loves going to work every day because once or twice a shift he's allowed to drive a giant red diesel truck as fast as he can. He loved racing cars as a kid. Now he loves racing fire trucks. It's what he was born to do."

Luis considers my tale. His long fingers are rinsing glasses, holding one up to the light now to check for smudges. "Your friend is a lucky man," he says. "Also a wise one, I think. He knew his purpose when he encountered her."

"How did he do that? Recognize it?"

"He realized it was a path with heart," Luis says. "For the injured, and people in fires, it is important that your friend drive fast and drive well."

"So because his purpose helps people in great need, it is a path with heart?"

"Si."

"Unlike our Mr. Bluefish," I say.

"Yes. Unlike our Mr. Bluefish." Luis slides the shot glasses into a wooden rack over his head. "Have you given thought to what happened tonight?"

"I'm trying to block it out."

"Do not," Luis says. "This is a serious matter."

I nod. "I know."

"This man Bluefish will almost certainly try to kill us. Perhaps not right away. He would be wise to wait, let us think he has kept his word."

"Sounds sneaky enough for Bluefish. Did you get a good look at that creep driving...before you changed the shape of his head, I mean?"

Luis ignores me, says, "We must make plans, take special care. Before this is over, we may decide killing Bluefish is our only protection."

I pull my wallet, find the yellow scrap of paper Mr. Vick gave me Friday night. I show Luis Tony's name and telephone number.

"Who is Tony?" Luis says.

"My boss said I should call him in case of trouble with his daughter. I did, and he took care of it. I bet he could take care of Bluefish, too."

Luis switches off the beer signs. "Is this Tony a lawyer? Or a thug like Bluefish?"

"I don't know."

"It is of little consequence, I think. This matter must be settled between us and Bluefish."

28

Luis is ready to close up. The old couple finishes their tea. I'm not sure, but I think Luis may have himself a steady girlfriend these days.

I slide off the barstool. "You mean you and Bluefish will settle it, Luis. I'm not much of a fighter."

Luis shakes his head. "This is not true, amigo. Myself, I am experienced with many weapons. My favorite is the switchblade, and I handle even the twelve-inch ones with great skill. Yet your words can be more cutting than my biggest knife. Austin Carr fights with his brain and his mouth. And he fights very well."

Now that's an interesting take on my Gift for Gab. I always saw my verbal proficiency as a shield, not a weapon. But who am I to argue with a Toltec warrior.

NINE

A year ago, I didn't have diddly-squat. I lived in a pickup-mounted camper. My wages were garnished. I was thousands of dollars in debt, including overdue alimony and child-support payments. The ex-wife even had a restraining order preventing me from seeing our children. Very little to lose in those days. Taking risks came smooth and easy.

Now my support payments—all my bills—are current. I get Ryan and Beth every Wednesday night for dinner and again every other weekend. I can afford a two-bedroom apartment and a leased Toyota. More important, my ownership interest in Shore Securities could fund my kids' college education, provided Carmela and I, the people we hire, run Shore as well as Mr. Vick did.

Point being, all of sudden I've got plenty to lose. That's why I'm pushing Brooklyn Tony on Bluefish. I have no idea what happened to Rags after Tony dragged him out of Shore's offices last week, but I know Rags hasn't bothered me or Carmela since. Maybe Tony can pull off the same kind of disappearing act with Bluefish.

Tony examines me standing on his porch with the soft, confident brown eyes of a German Shepherd. Calm, relaxed, just inside the threshold of his home in Graves End, Brooklyn, Mister Handsome extends his paw for me. "Come on in."

He practically lifts me inside with his giant mitt. Tony's got on an extra-extra-large gray golf shirt and navy sweats, but there's no missing the muscle beneath the loose cloth. This guy snatched me off the porch like I was the afternoon newspaper.

"Any trouble finding the place?" he says.

Across my shoulders, his hand weighs like a backpack loaded for an assault on Everest.

"No problem," I say. "And I really appreciate you seeing me. I'm a little embarrassed coming for dinner."

Tony's body hardens like fast-drying glue. "Embarrassed?" His brown eyes narrow into a glare that fills my blood with adrenaline. Jesus. Is that what they call the prison stare? "What?" he says. "You got a problem coming to Grave's End?"

Yipes. "Hell, no. I mean embarrassed about putting you out. Making your wife cook for me. I would have been happy to take you and the wife—"

"Oh."

"—out to dinner."

Using his hand like a puppeteer, Tony twists both our heads to greet a dark-haired young woman striding our way. She's wearing a black skirt and a furry, sleeveless sweater with yellow and black horizontal stripes.

"Is this Vick's friend Austin?" she says.

Tony saying, "My wife Gina."

Mrs. Tony Farascio is a knockout. Long midnight hair, maybe ten or twelve inches past her shoulders. Huge, oval, yellow-flaked brown eyes. An ear-to-ear smile whose sincerity appears generated by an even bigger heart. The smile and the striped sweater remind me of honey bees and summer days. Sweet stuff, this Gina.

She offers her hand. "Austin."

I give her the full-boat Carr grin when her fingers brush mine. I feel dizzy, spinning in a field of perfumed July flowers. Hey, wake up, Carr. Time to snap out of Gina's spell before I erect myself a tower of trouble.

"Can I get you a drink?" she says.

"But Carmela's doing okay?" Tony says. "That prick Ragsdale was a serious loser."

"Was?"

"Slip of the tongue. I took him to the 'splaining department is all, told him what might happen if he ever showed up again at Vick's place."

I nod, wondering if my boss Vick picked up the 'splaining department joke from Tony, or visa versa. "Great. Thanks. No, Carmela's doing fine. It's this other thing with Bluefish why I called."

Tony and I sip after-dinner sambucas in the Farascio's downstairs playroom, a tennis-court-size basement with two bowling lanes, a pool table, a card table, a mini-theater with a big screen TV and recliners for eight, a juke box, a soda fountain, and enough cushioned perimeter seating for the Rutgers marching band.

"But you said Bluefish agreed to keep his end of bargain?" Tony says. "I don't see the problem."

"Neither I nor Luis trust him."

Tony's teeth crunch one of the three coffee beans floating in the sambuca. "I don't personally know this guy Bluefish, but I heard of him. I don't see him getting where he is in this world without keeping his word."

"Even with people he's about to kill?"

Tony grins. "You got a point there, pal."

Gina calls from the top of stairs. "Telephone, Tony."

I can't see her, but I definitely remember what the touch of her hand did to my heartbeat, the circulation in my extremities. Her voice makes me almost smell her.

Tony stands. "Let me check out a few things," he says. "I'll get back to yah."

TEN

Mama Bones saying, "Why you no tell me?"

I wedge the phone against my ear, freeing my hands to sign a stack of checks Carmela's presented me. We're busy at Shore today, the guys scoring big working Walter's accounts. Don't tell those A.A.S.D. jerks who suspended my license, but I've been helping Shore's bond desk fill orders and racking up a few commission dollars myself. My trades get routed through a phony rep number.

"Hey, I'ma talking here," Mama Bones says.

Walter's doing the same—banging the phones—with Shore clients—our clients—whose names and phone numbers he swiped on the way out of here. The bastard. I heard twice today from customers that Walter called them, said Shore was bound to go broke, that we've already hired a bankruptcy lawyer. My pal, Walter.

"Hey," Mama Bones says.

I should have guessed. Stockbrokering is not a great vocation for maintaining tight personal friendships. I can't imagine what the business was like during the days of legal dueling.

"Hey, Golly Gee!" Mama Bones says. "Why you no tell me?"

I stop signing checks. Nobody's called me Golly Gee in a while. Not since I moved here from California and learned to curse like a New Jersey native. I move the phone closer to my mouth. "Mama Bones, I did just tell you. I called to see if you needed help with that bingo-game thing, and when you asked what happened when Bluefish came to Luis's on Monday, I—"

"Why you no tell me before you call Tony?" she says. "Is abada-bada mistake you ask this man to do something. He and his Brooklyn crew worse than Bluefish, worse than *gavones*. That Tony devil teach

33

my Vittorio abada-bada things."

"How did you know Bluefish threatened me at Luis's?"

"Lucky guess."

"Mama Bones?"

"I dunno. Maybe I have vision. Bye."

"Mama—?"

She's gone. Strange, as I said nothing to Carmela, Mama Bones's granddaughter. Although there were lots of people in Luis's restaurant the other day who saw what happened. Plus Mr. Vick's bragged many times about his mother's exercise-bookmaking business. Unless she's booking all the bets herself, she could be tied to, or even part of, Bluefish's gambling operation.

One thing I'm not buying is Mama Bones's voodoo vision theory.

Sixty-six percent of the time eating dinner with my kids on Wednesday night is one-hundred percent predictable. Ryan always picks Burger King. I invariably choose Luis's Mexican Grill. Only when it's Beth's turn might our evening involve actual culinary adventure. Tonight is such a night.

Beth saying, "Is this place cool or what?"

"Looks like Dracula's castle," Ryan says.

I brake for valet parking at the apex of a huge circular driveway. Two-story rhododendrons line the walkway and steps.

The Locust Tree Inn & Restaurant caters to foreign and gourmet tastes, and I should take advantage, try something exotic for dinner tonight. I hear, for instance, the tube steak rocks.

"Does this place have cheeseburgers?"Ryan says.

"Only dorks eat cheeseburgers every night," Beth says.

"Hey," I say. "Be nice."

The kids precede me up flagstone steps. One of Branchtown's earliest settlers snagged a fortune growing corn beside the Navasquan river, boating his crop to Manhattan. Four hundred years later, his three-story, thirty-room Tudor mansion remains the number one venue for weddings in Central New Jersey. And Wednesday through Sunday brunch, Branchtown's priciest restaurant.

Like her mother, my daughter has Old Money tastes.

Beth saying, "I'm cold."

"I've got the creeps, too," Ryan says. "Did you see that guy who brought us our Cokes?"

It is a little weird in here. We checked out the ten-pound leather menus, started with Diet Cokes, and just ordered our thirty-dollar entrees. We're still the only people eating.

"Do you have a jacket in the car?" I say to Beth.

"No. I thought this sweater would be warm enough, but it's so drafty in here."

"You picked this creep-o-rama," Ryan says.

"Shut up," Beth says.

"Be nice," I say.

I take off my suit coat and wrap Beth's shoulders. All four dining-room walls glow with dark, richly-oiled wood. Gargoyles with fangs, claws, and bulging angry eyes watch us from all four cornices of the ornamental, hand-plastered ceiling. Truthfully, the monsters look a little dusty.

"Really, Pop. Did you see that waiter?" Ryan says.

"He's just old," I say. "People's ears and noses never stop growing, you know. That's why almost everybody looks funny when they get old."

"You don't look funny," Ryan says.

Ouch. "Hey. I'm not old."

Ryan and Beth glance at each other and giggle.

Outside, two pine trees have grown extra-tall, and two perfectly spaced lights shine at me through the forest. Looking out the window, the effect reminds me of giant ears and huge yellow eyes. Like a four-story cat peering at me. I shudder. Maybe Ryan's right about this place. Creepy.

"What's the matter, Daddy?" Beth says.

"Guess I'm cold, too."

"I have to go to the bathroom," Ryan says.

Figures. One trip for every glass of Coke. "We passed the men's room on the way in," I say. "Near the front door."

"I'll be right back."

Ryan takes off at a brisk walk. Iced tea does that to me. Or maybe it's all liquids. I think the problem might be genetic as my old man was always using the toilet. Our family road trips were planned around the availability of clean public restrooms.

I watch Ryan tack toward the hallway. His shadow dances on

the wall a moment after he disappears. I'm about to turn away when a huge second shadow flashes across the same wall. My heart skips when I recognize the huge profile.

"Ryan!" I jump to my feet and run.

Beth calling, "Daddy, what's the matter?"

My daughter's frightened. Behind me, her wavering voice cuts me, makes me want to turn back and comfort her. But I can't. That second shadow looked like Bluefish's oversized driver, Max.

The Creeper.

ELEVEN

In the hallway just outside the dining room, I run into a charging rhinoceros. No wait. It's The Creeper, crushing me against the wall and emptying my lungs with his horn-like fist. I know rhinos are bigger and stronger than The Creeper, but it doesn't feel like it. Or maybe I was fooled by The Creeper's soiled, spotted gray coat. It smells like and otherwise resembles animal hide.

Probably a funny thing to notice when you can't breathe, but I think The Creeper's got that European perspective on bathing, too. You know, only sissies use soap.

"Get up," he says.

I'm sinking to the floor as he growls this. When my butt hits reaches bottom, I still can't grab a breath, let alone stand, and since I don't see or hear Ryan, I choose to stay right here on the hardwood floor, occupying The Creeper's creepy attentions.

Air surges into my lungs as rhino-man yanks me up by the belt, wraps his anaconda arm around me, and spins me horizontal. Holding me on his hip like a small rolled up rug. My lungs and spirit enjoy the newly reacquired air supply until I hear small footsteps in the hall.

"Pop?"

"Run, Ryan," I say.

Holding me with his right arm, Creeper jumps sideways and snatches Ryan with his left.

"Hey," Ryan says.

I feel like a beetle in the clutches of a six-year-old boy. Helpless and doomed.

My world view begins to bounce, my arm bumps a door jam,

and The Creeper delivers us like lost pets, one on each hip, back into the dining room. The huge chamber isn't empty anymore, though. Bluefish relaxes at my old table with Beth. His greasy fingers caress her hair.

My fingernails press into my palms. I'm all out of smart ass.

Every inch of the five-thousand-square-foot dining room smells like The Creeper's unwashed armpits. And I can't take my eyes off his nose. It has more bends than a toboggan run. I still want to kill Bluefish for touching my daughter's hair, but I realize now isn't the best time.

"Have I made my point?" Bluefish says. He glances at both of my children. Beth the oldest. Maybe Seaside County's best teenaged swimmer. And Ryan. My shortstop and Hardy Boys fan. My kids nibble their dinners at one table, Bluefish and The Creeper, at another. There's maybe twenty feet of distance between us. I wish it were twenty miles.

Where in the hell are the other diners? A waiter?

"I understand," I say. "The point is you're threatening my children."

For the kids, I'm forcing a smile. Playing relaxed. Showing them everything's fine. Both of them keep sneaking glances. How could they not? I have to pretend I'm just dining with an eccentric client who likes to wear black silk suits and eat with his creepy rhino-shaped bodyguard.

No sweat.

So far, Bluefish and Creeper are holding their voices and tempers down, going along with my client act. Although Creeper doesn't have to say or do much to make things look scary. The bandaged wound Luis put on his temple oozes blood. I hope it hurts like hell.

"My point is you can't protect them," Bluefish says. "Not twenty-four hours a day, not for one fucking minute if I choose otherwise."

"I get it," I say. My hands ache to snatch this bastard's slicked-back hair and rip off his scalp. Instead, I'm saying, "I'll open your account personally."

I force myself to bite into my prime rib dinner, and then beg my jaws to chew. See Ryan, Beth? Everything's fine. I glance again at

Bluefish's temptingly long, grip-able hairdo, but I've got no real options as far as I can see. Getting Beth and Ryan home safely can be my only priority.

"Good," Bluefish says. "In the trunk of your car you'll find a red gym bag with one-hundred-thousand in cash and a signed Shore Securities account application. Buy me big cap, big name stocks."

"All right," I say. "Blue chips for Bluefish."

I hand the valet his tip with a shaky hand and slide in behind the wheel of my Camry. Because of the wide market for its parts, America's best-selling automobile is also the country's most stolen. Wish someone would steal my Camry with Bluefish's money in the trunk.

"Okay, Pop, we're in the car," Ryan says. "So who were those men?"

Both kids buzzed me with questions when Bluefish and The Creeper abandoned us in the dining room. I told them we needed to scram, that I'd answer questions when we got to the car. I needed time to think.

Beth saying, "Daddy?"

"They're friends of Mr. Vick's," I say. "The one named Bluefish is mad Vick went away and left me in charge at Shore Securities."

"Is that why that big creepy guy picked us up like puppies?" Ryan says.

Internally, I can admire my son's eye for detail. He's got Bluefish's driver pegged.

"Max is a little rambunctious," I say. "Like a big kid."

The quiet in the back seat indicates a certain skepticism, I suppose, but in this case I think lies are superior to the truth.

Beth says, "Daddy, are those men like the people who tried to kill you last year? Criminals?"

The best lies, however, always offer a bit of truth.

"Maybe, I don't know. But it doesn't matter. Bluefish isn't mad anymore."

"He didn't exactly look happy," Ryan says.

Like I said, Ryan's got an eye for detail.

"If you had to ride around in a car with that smelly guy Max, would you be happy?"

Bouncing into my ex-wife Susan's driveway ten minutes later, breaking a long silence, Ryan asks if he and Beth need to go into the FBI's witness protection program.

"No," I say. "But I'll need to if you tell your mother about this."

TWELVE

The next day after work I find Luis's Mexican Grill in the full-boat grip of rigor mortis. Subdued voices, no laughter. The light crowd focuses either on oval plates of Umberto's semi-famous enchiladas and tacos or CNN's pretty-face actress blaring death estimates for another Baghdad bombing. The air tastes brittle, ready to crack.

A stranger might think America's war with radical Islam and Saddam Hussein loyalists was to blame for this pall, but I can see the cause is much more personal. Armed violence threatens the home front as well. I don't recognize him as being among Luis's friends, but another Toltec warrior pins me from under Luis's caballista sombreros. Within reach of the stranger's big paws, a tall brown package leans against his barstool. Could be a couple of golf clubs. Maybe one of those thin, fungo baseball bats. Then again, the shape reminds me a whole bunch more of a single-barrel, pump-action shotgun.

No wonder the joint's tense.

Luis is busy making drinks. He takes a few minutes to spot me, Luis collecting money and mixing big pitchers of margaritas. Soon as our eyes lock though, my favorite bartender/club owner wipes his hands on a white towel and struts my way, Luis jaunty, but tense, too, the swagger contained.

He snatches at my offer of a handshake. Wow. The restaurant's atmosphere isn't the only thing uptight around here. Luis's shiny black eyes bear the resolute, defensive wariness of a big-city cop walking up beside your car. One hand on his holster.

Whatever Luis's problems, mine are worse. I decide to file a formal complaint. "Bluefish threatened my children, Luis. He brought that creep-ass giant with him, too, surprised me, Ryan, and Beth at the restaurant. Bastard had me roughed up in front of my kids."

Luis's eyes briefly shut. A long, slow blink. He says, "Did you agree to do him the favor?"

I nod. "I couldn't say no."

"What about this man Tony?"

"I haven't heard from him since the day before yesterday."

Luis reaches low to his left, draws up a half-full bottle of Herradura Gold and pours us two shots. "It is lucky for me I have not yet fathered children. I have only myself and the restaurant to protect."

My friend doesn't know the half of it. Besides Beth and Ryan, my current security responsibilities include Carmela, Shore Securities, and Mama Bones. Thanks to my boss and market mentor, Mr. Vick, I'm sworn to protect his, mine, and ours. Where's my badge? My troops? Where's Tony?

"I noticed the guy with the shotgun," I say. "I assume he's a friend of yours."

Luis ignores my implied question. He wraps two fingers around his shot glass, drinks his Herradura and sneaks a glance at the front door. Maybe he thinks I'm guessing, that his armed pal remains obscure.

I throw back my own tequila. Tilt my head in the guard's direction. "I admit I'm nervous looking. I have to go see the A.A.S.D. lady in a few minutes. But, come on, Luis. That guy pinned me like an owl on a field mouse when I walked in. And that brown paper package beside him is about as subtle as a bazooka."

He shakes his head. "Then Bluefish's spy will easily pick him out as well."

"Count on it."

He pours us another shot. "I must make my friend less visible."

I glance at the hombre beneath the sombreros. "And maybe get a couple more friends."

I park in the Martha Washington Inn's side lot, grab my coat, and slide out of the Camry. A putrid, river-bottom odor whacks my nose. Branchtown residents have been throwing nasty things in the

Navasquan River for more than four-hundred years. The gifts return in spirit every low tide.

I breathe as shallowly as possible walking to the hotel's main entrance. The Martha Washington Inn perches on a small bluff overlooking the river, the hotel's whitewashed wooden exterior molting away like feathers from an ancient seagull.

Cool and clear this evening in Central New Jersey. A few clouds glow pink in the west. Not a bad night to roost at the Martha's upstairs brass and mahogany bar, watch the sun go down. After dark, lights pop on in the big river estates, throwing sparklers onto black water.

Maybe after I meet with the A.A.S.D.'s Anne Marie Talbot, I'll have a Bombay martini and check out the lights.

"Hey. Carr."

I let go of the Martha's front glass door and swivel to see who's called my name. It's Tony Farascio, all six feet of him, the stubble on his George Clooney cheeks thick and black as coal dust.

"Hey, Tony. What's up?"

"I decided to help you with that other thing."

Tony sticks out his hand. He's wearing tan cotton slacks, new white sneakers, and another extra-big, short-sleeve knitted green golf shirt beneath an unzipped Navy blue London Fog wind breaker. I'm familiar with his big hands, that crunching grip, but as he walks toward me I notice Tony also owns exceptionally light feet for a big man. Like a pro defensive lineman.

We drop the shake. "Carmela told you I was going to be here?" I say.

"Yeah."

"Well, I don't need any help with the A.A.S.D. But I sure could have used you last night. Bluefish threatened my children."

Tony slams a forefinger to his lips. "Wait a minute," he says. He guides me inside the Martha's lobby, then off to a quiet corner beside a thirty-gallon blue Chinese vase filled with blooming yellow flowers.

"Sorry, pal," he says. "But I didn't think Bluefish would make his move that fast. Plus, I had to get permission. But I'm on it now."

I nod.

"I heard about the cash he gave you," Tony says.

"You did? From who"

"I got friends in Bluefish's family. All over, in fact. You still have his money?"

"Yes."

Tony smiles and wraps a thick arm around my shoulders. "Let's go have a pop at the bar. You can tell me about this A.A.S.D. problem."

"I don't have time. The A.A.S.D. woman is waiting for me now. She just came into town today on a fluke and agreed to meet me. So it's important. I don't want to be late."

He shrugs and redirects me toward the elevators. "Okay, let's go see her. We'll have a pop later."

Once again I resist his forward momentum. Like before, my shoes slide on the slick marble. "You can't go with me," I say.

"Sure I can. You're going to need me."

He plows another few steps toward the elevators, me scuffing along with him. Suddenly he brings us both to a halt. "Wait. I got an idea. Let's go back to your car, get Bluefish's money. We might need that, too."

My heart rate ticks up a notch. "What are you talking about? What's Bluefish's money got to do with the A.A.S.D.? Jesus, Tony. You'll get Shore closed down letting her see all that cash. Like I'm trying to bribe her."

"Her name's Anne Marie Talbot, right?"

"Yeah. So?"

"And if she files her report with co-mingling charges included, Shore Securities gets hurt bad?"

"Probably. But—"

"So trust me, Carr. Vick told you to ask for my help, right?"

"Yeah, but there's no way Mr. Vick would want you to bribe her. Jesus."

Tony tows me through the glass doors, back outside. Once more, the gooey, tongue swelling smell of dead fish punches me in the nose. Tony's arm, the odors, fear suddenly pumping up my heart rate— feels like I'm about to faint.

Mr. Brooklyn checks my face, shakes his head. "You look upset."

There's no way I can stop Tony Farascio from doing whatever the hell he wants. If I try to muscle him, I'll end up as rotting goo, reeking like the other poor souls paving the Navasquan River bottom.

"When you give me Bluefish's money, I think I gotta go see this

44

BIG MONEY

Anne Marie by myself," Tony says.

My jaw drops. Joining my series seven license, my Gift of Gab turns temporarily suspended.

I am freaking speechless.

THIRTEEN

Max stares at Anne Marie on the tiny black and white recording monitor. Look at her, rubbing that silly deodorant on her shaved armpits. Powder on her crotch. Now pulling those see-through black panties on her ass.

He should ask Jerry for a bigger screen. Maybe one of those big plasma televisions like Jerry just bought for his apartment.

Max completes another set of one-hundred push-ups. He rolls onto his back for a set of sit-ups, but swaps his head for his feet so he can watch Anne Marie finish dressing. Hooking lace bra under her pillowy breasts; stuffing her soft flesh and into those small cups.

What would she do if he went next door right now, to her hotel room?

He sighs. Maybe she's the woman to take Max away from this life. Anne Marie has been very nice to him, that's for sure, like Jerry says. She has sex with him almost anytime he wants. Even cooks dinner for him once in a while.

He checks the lights on the recording equipment, just like Jerry showed him. Red and blue. Gauges okay. Everything is good, working fine. Jerry and the rest of Bluefish's boys will be lining up to watch this tape.

Max wipes the sweat off his forehead, stands, and then bends at the waist, hands on his thighs. He takes a long slow breath. Then another.

He glances at the monitor. Bluefish says Anne Marie doesn't know about the camera. But the way she's playing with her breasts, she has to know she's being watched.

She looks like she's putting on a show.

Max unzips his pants.

FOURTEEN

I extend my tongue full length, French-kissing my third martini. The now-empty, nearly clean conical glass winks back at me, another subtle indicator of full-boat overindulgence. Could this martini-glass warning blinker—a lighthouse perched above the jagged coastline of reality—suggest my ineligibility for a fourth see-through?

My only hesitation in leaving the bar involves a strawberry blonde. She's sitting on a nearby stool—we're upstairs at the Martha—and, more important, the lady seems to like my looks. Grinning at me in a very particular way. I have the feeling if I stay right here, drinking and winking, Cutie Pie with an Edge may just wander over here and rub me up. She's got that "I do whatever the hell I want" line etched into her chin.

Logic, Shore's business, and my children's college education luckily snag hold of my over-sexed, gin-rotted brain. Checking the bartender's watch, I see Brooklyn Tony's been up in Talbot's room more than an hour. If he's trying to bribe that woman from the American Assn. of Securities Dealers, Tony could put Shore out of business, maybe install my pink ass in a white-collar prison. The U.S. District Attorney in Trenton loves to make an example of corporate criminals.

I throw down thirty bucks and slide off my stool. I must be nuts letting Tony go up to Talbot's room, let him represent Shore Securities with the A.A.S.D. What was I thinking? At the very least I should have held out as long as physically possible, let the contusions and concussions speak later of my attempt to prevent Tony's madness.

Besides Carmela, who walked in ten minutes ago, the Martha's bar swells with lingering sunset gazers and silver-haired seniors ordering early-bird specials from the bar menu. Through the crowd, the strawberry blonde and I find each other's gaze.

I only snag a glimpse on my way out, but Strawberry's wearing a scooped-neck black dress that frames her breasts and drapes her hips like liquid chocolate. Diamond earrings twinkle at me, but not as brightly as the lady's smile. If Johnny Depp the pirate had a blonde sister...

I wave and disappear into the elevator lobby.

Figures. Probably the love of my life back there, and I'm ditching the bar and a chance to meet her because everything I have, everything my children need, could be sliding down the big financial drain as I speak.

The room tilts. Oops. I shouldn't have gone for the martini quatro. The third one buried me anyway.

The elevator doors rattle open before I push the button and Tony's wife Gina the Luscious almost crashes into me rushing out. What the hell's she doing here? Her shoulder-length black hair dangles loose and uncombed. Her cashmere sweater sports a torn seam across the right shoulder. And Gina Farascio's gorgeous face is drawn tight, her mascara smeared by tears.

The instant I catch her shoulders, preventing our collision, the lights go off and the Martha's fire alarm fills the hall with high-pitched electronic screaming. The piercing, throbbing whine stabs at my ears, the ugly noise somehow louder in the dark.

In a wash of red light, Gina's eyes go wide and wild. An intense red beacon flashes above us from high in the elevator lobby—the alarm's screaming now has a frightening visual quality.

The good news, if I have my bearings right in the semidarkness, the flashing red light locates the stairway. Escape. My heart's drumming.

It figures that lives are at stake. I've got five or six ounces of Bombay Sapphire in me, not to mention the vermouth. Plus—let's see if I can put this delicately—my brain's missing some blood thanks to Gina being so close. Like an airline's overhead baggage compartment, my contents have shifted.

A crowd of alarm-driven bar patrons streams into the small elevator lobby. The elevators lock shut. I reach for Gina's hand as the swelling pack of panicked seniors herds toward the stairs. I don't see or smell any smoke, but Gina and I don't have a choice. We're swept up like leaves in a water-filled gutter.

I slip my arm around her waist to keep us together.

Outside in the parking lot, Gina and I huddle with two or three dozen other elderly bar patrons, hotel guests, and staff while two Branchtown fire crews rush inside the Martha. I don't spot Tony, Ms. Strawberry, or Anne Marie Talbot anywhere in the crowd, but Carmela's out here. She's talking with three young women and a uniformed cop.

FIFTEEN

Gina Farascio's unruly gaze fixes on two Branchtown police cruisers bouncing into the Martha's parking lot. Behind the black-and-whites, I recognize Detective James Mallory's dirty brown Ford Fairlane. He hits the driveway at thirty miles an hour.

I'm guessing Branchtown's Bravest found something inside the Martha of serious interest to Branchtown's Finest. Arson? Or maybe somebody got burned.

Another half-hour goes by and we're still not back inside. The number of people waiting to return has dwindled considerably, no doubt a casualty of alcoholic thirst. I could use another see-through myself. In fact, I'd head back to Luis's if it wasn't for Tony and Bluefish's one-hundred-thousand cash. Oh, my.

I'm beginning to consider final resting spots.

"Carr."

Detective Mallory stalks me from behind. He has two uniformed officers beside him and a tense, don't-screw-with-me expression on his rosy face.

Actually, the only time Mallory doesn't have that nasty cast on his face is when he's coaching Little League baseball. Even then he talks to the kids like the umpire instead of a coach.

He grips my arm. "Talk to me, pal. Over there, by the patrol car."

Mallory tugs me over, hands on, like he's dragging a convict up before the judge. He nudges me against the black-and-white's rear fender and pushes his face up close. I think he might have had a beer with lunch. Sam Adams? Our noses are almost touching.

"Know a woman named Anne Marie Talbot?" he says.

Gulp. "Yeah." Mallory's eyebrows snap higher. I can almost feel wind. "She's an investigator with the American Association of Securities Dealers," I say. "She's been auditing Shore."

"Did you see her today?"

"No."

"You sure? I found your name on a pad by her telephone."

Double gulp. Why was Mallory up in Talbot's room? My stomach begins to fill with battery acid. Is there a criminal reason why I haven't seen Tony or Talbot?

"I had an appointment but didn't go," I say.

Mallory grins. Now his breath smells like gasoline. Maybe he was drinking brandy. "You're a bad liar, Carr. You expect me to believe you're at her hotel, but you didn't keep that appointment?"

"I don't care if you believe me or not. It's the truth. I sent an associate to keep my appointment."

Oh, my, that was dumb. Sometimes my gift of blab just means I have a big mouth.

"Yeah? And who would that be?" Mallory says.

I suck a big breath. Considering what Tony was carrying, and what he may have been doing with it, I'm not the smallest bit anxious to reveal Tony Farascio's identity. Or Shore's semiserious A.A.S.D. troubles. Oh, man, when am I going to learn to keep my trap shut?

I stall. "Tell me what's going on. Why all the questions?"

Mallory's right hand jumps up and pinches my shoulder. I feel like knocking it away. "Who went to see her, Carr? Tell me."

If people exercised the right to remain silent, our prisons would be empty. Too bad so many of us figure this out too late. I say, "You want me to say another word, Jim, explain what's happened. My lawyer's phone number is programmed into my cell phone."

His intense gaze holds onto mine, trying to intimidate me. Fat chance, Jimbo. I watched you throw baseballs all one summer. I've seen stronger arms on a Queen Anne chair.

Mallory saying, "Your five o'clock appointment was canceled, Carr. Anne Marie Talbot is dead."

SIXTEEN

Mallory's words smack me. Not as hard as the Creeper did last night, but enough to provoke the physical reaction I'm sure the Cop with the Girl Scout Arm hoped for. I feel my eyes go big, like silver dollars. When my breath comes back, it's quicker and a little shallow.

"Who did you send up there, Carr? Tell me now or I'm taking you in on suspicion of murder. Let the newspapers and TV stations have the news."

I labor for a deep breath. I need oxygen. I need the Lone Ranger. The Cisco Kid. Luis.

Okay, Carr, think quick. Tony Farascio is Mr. Vick's friend. Tony's carrying one-hundred-thousand dollars in what I assume to be unlaundered gambling money. And any way you look at it, thanks to me, Tony went to see Talbot on Shore's behalf. I do not want to give Mallory Tony's name.

Mallory screams at me. "Who the fuck was it?"

But Shore's troubles can only blossom into full-boat disaster if I lie during a murder investigation, play hide-the-truth with Branchtown cops.

When you're sinking in heavy shit, it figures as pure folly to dig yourself in deeper.

"His name's Tony Farascio," I say.

"Spell it."

"F-A-R-A-S-C-I-O."

"He works for you?"

"He's a friend of Mr. Vick's."

"He's a lawyer or something?"

"Something," I say. "Maybe just a friend."

Mallory's eyes narrow. "But he was on Shore Securities business?"

"I guess."

I didn't think it possible, but the tall cop pushes closer. His nose brushes mine. An Eskimo kiss.

Gee, Jim, does this mean we're going steady?

"Was he or wasn't he, Carr? I thought you were running the company while Vick's out of town."

I cough to clear my throat. That backs the bastard up. Maybe I should tell him I have TB.

"Mr. Vick told me to call Tony if I had trouble with..." My sentence dies. I'm wandering down a dangerous path here. I keep talking this way, explaining myself, it's going to sound like I—or Vick, Shore, somebody—hired Tony Farascio to threaten or even kill Talbot.

"Trouble with what?"Mallory says.

"Just trouble."

Mallory shakes his head. His jaw sets like black-flecked white marble. "Screw this, Carr. You're coming back to the station, spend the night answering questions. For now, just tell me what Farascio looks like."

The New Jersey sun is long gone. Stars flicker above the Navasquan River. I don't see Gina the Luscious anymore, and the last stranglers have wandered back inside the Martha. The Branchtown Fire Department rumbles from the parking lot in a red parade of trucks. Everything's finished. Especially me.

"Six foot one or two," I say. "Two hundred pounds. Dark wavy hair and a permanent five o'clock shadow. Handsome as a movie star."

"Eye color?"

"Brown. Like a puppy dog."

An hour later, at the police station, I say, "Listen to me. Every night our back office tells the clearing bank in New York what to do with the money and securities taken in during the day's business. We send the bank a list of names and account numbers, what's to be deposited in each."

Mallory and I sit in an eight-by-eight-foot police interview room with a desk and two chairs. The furniture ranked as old twenty-five years ago, and the puke green, chipped walls haven't been painted since Harry Truman was President. The floor smells of lemon disinfectant over stale urine.

"If the bank goofs," I say, "if they leave one dollar of a client's funds in Shore's catchall account, then technically we've co-mingled client moneys. And if we don't catch the mistake, if the banker doesn't bother telling us, just fixes it himself the next day, our permanent records become inaccurate."

Mallory nods with satisfaction. "I get it. And if this co-mingling charge hit the newspapers, Shore would lose a crap-load of business, maybe even close."

I nod my head.

"You or your boy Farascio killed Talbot to keep this report from going public," Mallory says.

He waves papers at me I assume came from Talbot's hotel room. How else would this redheaded Irish cop know about the co-mingling charges?

"Exactly," I say. "Shore hired Tony to kill the A.A.S.D. investigator because everybody knows a murder trial would make us look good."

"I don't think your friend Farascio expected to stand trial," Mallory says. "He figured to burn the place down, cover his tracks."

The interview room door opens and Mallory's partner leans in holding a manila envelope. The young detective looks nineteen in his schoolboy haircut and brand new J. C. Penny suit. Like an Eagle Scout.

"Here's the fax from Washington," Scoutboy says.

Mallory opens the folder, reads a few minutes while I wonder what he's staring at. I don't have a rap sheet, but maybe Tony does. Maybe I shouldn't have given up Farascio's name. I definitely shouldn't have let Tony go see Talbot. Mr. Vick's going to choke me when he gets back from Italy. Or, more likely, Tony, Bluefish, or Max will have throttled me long before the boss gets home.

If and when I get out of here, I'm never going to stop drinking martinis.

Mallory's had enough of the file. He tosses the manila folder onto the poetically inscribed table between us with a tiny splat. The papers and photos slide partially out, pulling my eyes like a Shania

Twain cheesecake calendar. What is this?

"How long have you and Anthony Farascio been friends?" Mallory says.

"I told you. We're not friends. I never met the guy until this week."

"Right. He's a total stranger. That's why you sent him up to deal with the A.A.S.D. for you."

"He's Vick's friend, not mine."

Mallory grins. His bony fingers pick up the manila folder again. He slides out a photo-fax, nudges the grainy image across the table. My open hand slides across the table to pick up the paper, the wood smooth against my fingertips. It feels like I'm crawling into a trap.

My eyes take in the shot of a burned-out, two-story brick building, probably a restaurant and bar judging by the blackened sign in the foreground that gives the joint's hours as 10 a.m. to 2 a.m. Guess it could be a massage parlor. One that knows how to give its customers the Big Finish.

Mallory saying, "The Feds call your pal Farascio 'Tony the Torch.'"

Huh?

Branchtown's top detective slides a second photo toward me, this one featuring three tarp-covered bodies, all with blackened feet peeking from under the canvas.

"He gets paid to burn things for insurance money," Mallory says. "Every once and a while, there are people inside. You people at the Martha tonight were lucky."

SEVENTEEN

A hard noise echoes inside my apartment. Rapping at the door. Who the hell needs me so badly at—I check the digital clock on my night stand—three o'clock in the morning? Mallory had enough of me by midnight. And it sure ain't Anne Marie Talbot. Is it wishful thinking to hope it might be Tony? With Bluefish's missing cash?

I slide out of bed. The toasted cheese smell of tomato pie lingers in my living room, but the sensation's not exactly pleasant. I stopped for eats on the way home from Branchtown's ancient brick police station and my stomach tells me I should have chosen lighter than Roman Ricco's greasy pizza. Ricco's idea of an olive oil drizzle resembles what's left in the pan after you fry a pound of bacon.

Bang, bang, bang. Can't be the Creeper. The front door would already be lying flat.

Peeking through a slit in the curtains, I see Gina Farascio huddled at my door. She's wearing the same torn sweater and wild eyes I saw at the Martha.

What I don't see until I open the door is Gina's handgun. She yanks some kind of shiny chrome revolver from her black purse, pushes it against my chest, and rushes me back inside.

"Where's Tony?" she says.

Her voice wavers with emotion. Fear or anger, I can't tell which. I've been too interested in her comely smell, the shape of her anatomy, that inner radiance shining from her eyes. And not in any particular order.

Gina kicks the door shut behind her. "Tell me where he is or I'll pull the trigger."

Where's Mallory when I need him? I'd even settle for the Eagle

57

Scout. "I don't know. I haven't seen Tony since about six. Before the fire."

The good news, Gina removes the revolver from my chest. The bad news, she lifts the gun's muzzle level with my nose. The ugly headline, her thumb cocks the hammer.

Judging by the large bore on this chrome puppy, I'm a few pounds per square inch away from decapitation.

"Turn around and walk me through the house," she says. "Slowly. No tricks."

Gina drops her lusciousness onto my leather couch and stuffs the gun back in her purse. "Sorry," she says. "I figured he'd be here."

Her huge brown oval eyes gaze intently at me. My fear turned quickly to anger when she lowered the weapon a minute ago, but now I feel like reaching out to embrace her. And it's more than just my groin talking. I want to soothe her soul. Honest.

"You have any scotch?" she says.

"Dewar's."

"Make it a double," she says.

Mrs. Tony Farascio's feeling better. She stretches her feet out on my couch and rattles her ice, sips what watery whisky remains, and nestles the now-empty drink into my carpet.

"Why were you with Tony at that hotel?" she says.

"Actually, he was with me. I had a meeting with the A.A.S.D. and Tony wanted to help."

Gina snorts. Like Tony might have had some other motive besides kindness. Gee, why didn't I think of that?

"What were you doing there?" I say.

"Following Tony. I know he's been cheating on me practically since the day we were married. I've just never actually caught him at it. If I could be one-hundred percent sure—find him just once in the sack—I'd have the strength to leave him."

I watch Gina push her shoes off, let them tumble to the floor. The black skirt rides up, showing me white thighs and making me dream higher. This is not a healthy or morally correct line of thought.

"The woman he went to see is an auditor with the American

Association of Securities Dealers," I say. "She's threatening to file a damaging report about my firm. I don't think he was up there cheating on you."

"You think Tony was in that woman's room on business?" she says.

"Yeah. She was in town to see me, not him."

Gina shakes her head at me like a scolding teacher, then reaches over her head for the light switch. "I'm sleeping on your couch tonight. I don't have to sleep with Tony's gun under my pillow, right?"

I stand up. "Right."

She flips off the light. "You're a nice guy, Austin, but you don't know shit."

I wake up the next morning hard at work on Gina's naked body. Only trouble, I'm dreaming. Gina's not sharing intimate touches. She's not sharing my bed. Mrs. Tony Farascio's not even in my apartment.

The blanket I gave her is neatly folded on the couch. The coffee machine still drips and a clean cup awaits me on the counter; the cup and a scribbled warning: "Make Tony tell you the truth."

EIGHTEEN

The truth about what?

That's the question I keep asking myself as I shower, smear Jif Chunky on wheat toast, and natty-up for work in a navy blue Canali, white button-down shirt, and a maroon tie embroidered with tiny gold clocks.

The Canali's secondhand, mind you. An unshaved, greasy-looking guy comes by the office every few months with a rack or two of little-worn expensive suits. Rumor is he buys them from recent Wall Street widows.

Wearing dead-man suits is as close to The Street as most Branchtown brokers will ever get.

Or maybe Gina's message—putting my suit aside for a minute—is just her way of tugging my chain about her unfaithful husband. Maybe her message is a kind of red herring. A MacGuffin. She could be so mad at Tony, so fed up with his cheating she won't believe a word the dumb bastard says.

Been there, done that. Wonder if Mrs. Tony Farascio's pissed enough to take a lover?

Not that I discerned any direct or indirect offers earlier this morning. I trust my instincts to have mentioned such sweet intelligence. Not that I'd even consider an affair with a married woman, mind you...although consideration is a tricky word. I'm not counting brief flashes of wicked fantasy.

I crank open the Camry's sky roof as I roll onto Shrewsbury Avenue. Except for parallel golden streaks of airplane condensation, a few puffs of pink cotton candy on the eastern horizon, the windy sky sets a clean palate for the coming day. The crystal air tastes like pine forests and snow-topped mountains.

I'm headed to work earlier than usual today, the sun still a yellow bulb playing peek-a-boo behind Branchtown's century-old sycamores and oaks. The kind of trouble I'm in—Bluefish threatening Ryan and Beth, Walter leaving, Talbot's charges, then her murder, Big Tony's wife giving me stiff ones—sleeping wasn't an option. My mind buzzes.

One good thing, an idea that came to me as I spread my peanut butter, I've decided to send Ryan and Beth away from Branchtown. By good, I mean they'll be safe. Missed but safe. My ex-wife Susan won't go along at first, but I think she'll cooperate after I describe Bluefish, The Creeper, and the stories about Anne Marie Talbot's body I overheard at the Branchtown Police station.

For twenty-four hours, I guess I figured Beth and Ryan would be safe as long as I did what Bluefish wanted. But Tony disappearing with the bookie's hundred grand, and Talbot's murder, definitely changes my assessment. Branchtown's turning ugly, especially for me and mine. Susan has to relocate our children someplace even I don't know about.

A man doesn't like to think he could be tortured into giving up his children's whereabouts. But why even take the chance? I'm a stockbroker, not special ops.

Crossing the train tracks, I glance across Broad Street toward Luis's Mexican Grill. Luis's and Umberto's cars are parked there every day except Monday, but I'm earlier than usual, curious if I've beat them to work.

Both cars are there, Umberto's fifteen-year-old Ford clunker and Luis's well-maintained red Jeep, but something else quickly grabs my eye. Something that kicks my heart into race mode. A fast-rising column of black smoke gushes from one of the restaurant's side windows.

Fire.

I have the Camry in a left turn anyway, so all I have to do is hold the wheel a little longer to snap a U across both northbound lanes of Broad Street. See how easy? Now my little Japanese import points right back into Luis's gravel parking lot. Who cares if a Branchtown cabby honks and shows me his middle finger?

I dig inside my coat for the cell phone as I bounce into the lot. The front suspension bottoms on the cement driveway, skids across the gravel. A double-boogie rhythm grabs hold of my heart.

The 9-1-1 lady takes my name and Luis's address, but I say no when she asks me to stay on.

"I'm going inside," I say.

Black smoke chokes the kitchen from ceiling to my waist, a solid hot mass, the line between black and clear a sharply defined slash across the rectangular space. The top of the long, food-prep table is already invisible.

I fall to my hands and knees and scurry like a rat along the wooden legs. Heat radiates on my back like the noon summer sun. My knees crack and shout with pain on Luis's imported Mexican tile.

Shit. I had to wear the Canali, right?

Umberto lies near the kitchen's twin stainless steel sinks he uses to wash vegetables. My fingers check the chef's pulse. The heartbeat feels strong and steady. I check around us, but there's no sign of Luis.

I grab Umberto's collar and drag him toward the back door. I duck walk to keep my head out of the smoke. Thank God the pint-sized Umberto doesn't weigh much more than Beth. I have him outside on the back steps before I can say roasted pablano chili.

He coughs. Breathing fine on his own.

Crawling back inside, I see the mass of hot black smoke engulfs the top three-quarters of the kitchen. I have to crouch lower than before, finally crawling, snaking along like some Marine recruit dodging barbed-wire.

The clean air tastes hotter than before, too. My lungs tell me to turn back.

I wheel right at the twin sinks on my way into the main dining room. My slacks begin to shred at the knees and elbows. Nobody's ever going to wear this imported puppy again.

The fire must have started in the basement. Flames almost eat me as I approach the burning cellar stairway. I push the door closed, blocking the flames, to make it past.

In the dining room, I see nothing on my right, but to the left, I spot a black Reebok poking out from behind the bar. Luis. I wriggle closer, the cloud of searing smoke warming my back like a red-hot poker.

I tug on his ankle but can't move him. I inch closer. My back feels like it's about to explode in flames. I grip him with both hands and yank. Nothing. He's stuck like a long-term investor.

NINETEEN

The smoke forces me down, the evil, hell-hot stuff stronger than The Creeper's hands. My nose is inches from the stained linoleum floor. A long gray bug with hundreds of synchronized legs runs for his life, tries hiding in my nostril. I snort to blow him away.

Maybe sniffing like that enhances the senses because suddenly I can smell the cotton-blend material of my suit warming to ignition.

Sirens blare on Broad Street. The floor begins to heat up like a pancake griddle.

I wiggle beside Luis to see what's snagging him. Whoa. No accident here. Luis's wrists are bound with rope and tied to the stainless steel leg of his four-hundred-pound ice maker. No time to untangle knots. I need a sharp edge.

I spasm a cough. Smoke fills my throat and makes me cough again. Dizziness blurs my vision. Probably the first stage of carbon monoxide poisoning.

My heart's skipping rope as I yank Luis's new switchblade from his right back pocket.

I hack at the ropes.

But I run out of air before I can free him.

My lips kiss the floor, searching for the smallest taste of oxygen. I cough again, then choke. Maybe getting a spoonful of air. No matter. Smoke fills the restaurant, floor to ceiling. That has to be my last breath inside this burning coffin.

Praying adrenaline will help, I finally slash the rope in two. I jerk Luis's body from underneath the bar and onto my shoulder. I stagger, reel backward under his weight, but the bar backs me up. I stay on my feet. This is it. Get out now. I can't take a breath and I can't stop walking.

Reminds me of my marriage to Susan somehow. I never liked any of the choices she offered.

Through the black rolling smoke and heat, I stumble past the basement stairway, bank left off the twin sinks, then grope along the kitchen's wooden table. My lungs want to burst.

My head and shoulders begin to outrun my feet, stealing my balance. I can't see my nose in the blackness.

My right hip bumps the last corner of the kitchen table, then empty space, and I pitch Luis and myself toward a memory of the back door. My shoulder crashes something hard, and I spin onto steps, stumbling enough to lose Luis and fall.

Luis lands in the sturdy arms of a Branchtown fireman.

Nobody bothers to catch me.

It's early afternoon before the nurses let me in to see a very woozy Luis. The smoke and fire did some minor damage to his lungs, but it's the concussion that's going to keep him in the hospital at least over night. The doctors think someone hit him with a pipe.

"What do you mean you can't do it?" I say. "You have to do it, Susan. Bluefish threatened them. Now he tried to kill Luis."

"So you claim," my ex-wife says. "But your word doesn't count for much."

"I would never lie about our children. How can you even think that?"

"Where am I going to send them, Austin? Disney World? Both my parents are sick. It's too late to book a sitter for the weekend. And I was counting on you picking them up tomorrow. I've got plans. You can't decide to back out at the last minute."

"That's what you think? This story is bullshit just to get out of taking my weekend with them?"

"It's the kind of thing an unreliable person like yourself would do."

I take a breath. And another.

"Austin?"

"You going to be home for a while?" I say.

"I'm picking up the kids at school in twenty minutes."

"I'll try to have someone else call you."

"Yeah? Who, Carmela? Your secretary?"

"How about Detective Jim Mallory?"

Don't know exactly what my B.P.D. connections earned Susan in the way of clarification, but I hear later somebody convinced her to swallow my idea. Mallory or a patrolman on Mallory's orders must have explained why I couldn't know where the kids were headed, either. Otherwise I'm sure Susan would have called me.

Ha ha.

TWENTY

In Vick's old office, I touch a sterling picture frame with strange reverence. Not sure why I left hanging this mid-ocean action photo of Mr. Vick's forty-four-foot motor yacht, the "Triple-A." Don't need visual reminders of my mortality, how close death by drowning came last year. But maybe I relish how much boats like this cost, how much money Mr. Vick made all those years as sole owner of Shore Securities. See, with room and board, figure I'll need half-a-million for Beth's and Ryan's college education, and it's always good to have hope. Especially in the midst of Shore's latest tornado.

Except for the yacht shot, most of the rest of the boss's office crap has pretty much disappeared, casualties of an unbending policy: The Austin Carr Touch, currently amplified I'm sure by the key to Mr. Vick's well-stocked, well-heeled, and normally well-locked mahogany liquor cabinet. My motto after two weeks of many forty-year-old double-bourbons: Make yourself at home.

A fold-up card table with a nifty Swedish coffee drip machine, straw baskets of sweeteners, nondairy creamer, spoons, paper cups, and napkins replaces Mr. Vick's antique glass-front lawyer's bookcase.

If I want to read books, I can go to the library.

A longer, rectangular fold-up table bumps Vick's ten-ton cluttered desk. Three black trash bags full of knickknacks—Vick can't remember what his family looks like?—gives me enough room for a cushy swivel chair, four eighteen-inch computer monitors, three state-of-the-art laptops, and a laser printer that could publish the *Washington Post*. Plus, I can slide my chair underneath and back and forth along the whole table, do four internet dating applications and interviews at the same time.

Just kidding.

The paneled wall's invisible closet holds half my suits, half my dress shirts, drawers of socks and underwear, and a rack of suitably-conservative neckties. All this so I can dress here or at home, depending on mood, circumstance, and the number of elapsed hours since my latest adventure inside a flaming restaurant.

If this means an occasional wee-bity pile of dirty, smoky laundry, it's exactly the kind of necessary office evil Austin Carr can live with. Function, not form, is another one of my mottoes, bourbon or no.

The intercom buzzes. Nasty noise, that. Another Mr. Vick leftover I could do without.

I touch the black button. "Carmela, after you call the hospital about Luis, call the electrician for me, will you? I want this intercom—"

"Your appointment is here," Carmela says.

"It's four-thirty already?"

My new partner sighs. The sound is breathy and sexy. "It's five-forty-five," Carmela says. "You told me to set it up after work, right?"

I sign off my AOL account. This new dating site offers no one worth chasing. Hope I didn't click myself into the annual membership. I do remember typing in my credit card number. "This appointment is the big hitter from Jaffy Ritter Clark?" I say.

"Yup."

"Frank something?"

"Franny Dahler," Carmela says. "This hitter's a female. Did over eight hundred last year."

"Oh, my."

"Right. Should I send her in?"

Talking all day, working her dad's accounts and helping field my calls, Carmela's voice grows huskier each day. Sends a low lovely tingle deep in my waist. Jesus, I'm so horny even Miss Butterface is starting to arouse me. Well, everything but her face.

"By all means," I say. "Send in Ms. Dahler."

I swear I'm not really cruel. It's my endless search for sarcasm that leads me astray. Besides, Carmela can't hear what I'm thinking.

"Hire her," Carmela says.

Mr. Vick's daughter has been hurling little tips on running the business my entire two weeks as chief. Even before I ransacked Mr. Vick's office. I think the busty new college graduate's heady with power, although it can't hurt to listen. She already came up with one idea that clicked like the trunk of a new Mercedes: Firing Mr. Vick's crabby, overpaid secretary was a slash of genius.

What do we care if she's Vick's sister?

I stand to greet the hitter from across the street, Franny Dahler. She's been calling since Monday, one week after Walter left us for Dahler's current employer, Jaffy Ritter Clark. According to Carmela, Ms. Dahler wants to talk about switching firms.

Bet Jaffy Ritter gave her office to Walter.

My door cracks open.

The loss of Walter's production hurts Shore badly. And not just in profits for the owners. Shore Securities needs a certain flow of business to justify four back-office people, three secretaries, and two traders, not to mention minimum clearing fees with a New York bank and fifty other expenses included in the cost of selling stocks, bonds, and mutual funds. Peoples' jobs depend on me lining up a new hitter to pick up Walter's slack.

The door swings open. Oh. My. God.

"You're Austin Carr?" Ms. Strawberry says.

TWENTY-ONE

Ms. Strawberry saying, "I'm insulted you don't remember me."

I give Cutie Pie the full-boat Carr grin. Either I'm a better liar than even I thought—impossible—or this reddish-blond-haired stockbroker is pulling all three of my legs. No way Ms. Strawberry didn't notice I was staring at her like hungry crabs at a sick fish. "That's not what I said. More like, this woman is so incredibly attractive, she can't be real."

Ms. Strawberry doesn't blush or blink. Instead, she crosses her legs, showing me enough thigh to arouse a dead man. Wonder if producing boners is how she grossed $800,000 last year? She certainly has all the qualifications for leadership. Put Ms. Strawberry in a corporate boardroom, they'd elect her chairman and chief executive. When they voted, more than hands would go up.

"Perhaps your assessment was blurred by too many martinis," she says.

I roll my chair up close to the desk. Don't think Ms. Dahler's quite ready for a complete frontal view of my lap just yet. My appreciation for her thin summer dress is quite formidable.

"Perhaps I was over-served," I say. "I did have a lot on my mind."

"You mean Shore's A.A.S.D. troubles?" She grins, a startling display of pure white, perfectly capped teeth. Another movie-star-quality ranking for Ms. Strawberry's physical nature.

Wait. How did she know about the A.A.S.D. investigation? Was Ms. Strawberry close enough last night to hear me talking to myself? No, wait...I know what happened.

"Walter mentioned the A.A.S.D. investigation around Jaffy

70

Ritter?"

Ms. Strawberry nods, bouncing her chin-length, wavy blonde hair. "More like he gave lectures on the subject. To me and regular luncheon crowds."

Sounds like Walter. The bastard. I thought we were pals, so I kept his departure secret two days. Meanwhile, he used that weekend to work on Shore's client list, including two of my biggest clients. When I lived in California, I might have talked about hurt feelings. In Jersey, we say Walter made me his bitch.

"So why would you want to move to Shore?" I say. "There could be bad publicity, plus you know Shore can't afford the kind of bonus a big wire firm could pay. Right now, Shore can't afford to pay any kind of bonus."

Let's see how she handles obstacles. And in case she jumps this puppy, I've got another one growing in my pants. It's nature, ladies. Survival of the species.

Franny's gaze searches mine, then holds me tight. Her chin's set, too. Like the larger, vertical keystone of a brick window arch. "I don't want a big bonus," she says. "I want a bigger percentage of commissions and mutual fund trailers."

Okay, that figures. Franny Dahler, alias Ms. Strawberry, the Nicole Kidman of Branchtown, knows Shore Securities might flounder without Walter. She's trying to seize me by the short hairs.

Strawberry saying, "And I'm willing to stick long enough to make the deal pay off for both of us."

I glance at my empty bourbon glass. I like this blonde lady. And I mean over and above my not-so-secret lust. I know she can sell, for one thing. I know I'd never say no to her. Damn. All of which means I'm probably going to let her squeeze my nuts. My only real hesitation, I sense Ms. Strawberry's not telling me everything about her desire to change firms. It's more than money. Swear to God, I'll bet Walter got her corner glass office overlooking the Navasquan River. Something like that.

"How about fifty percent for five years?" I say.

But white lies and hunches can't matter in Shore's current situation. Once I start letting back-office people go, I'll lose more salesmen. Could become an ugly cycle. Mr. Vick will return next fall to find me and Carmela working in a camper with cell phones.

"How about sixty for three?" she says.

It's strictly business me wanting to hire her. I'm paying absolutely no attention to whatever is lifting my makeshift desk. The table with three computers and four monitors on it.

"Fifty-five percent is the best I can do, Franny. And that's if you'll sign a contract for four years."

"Commissions and mutual fund trailers?"

"Everything."

"Done," she says.

I stand in my enthusiasm to shake hands on the deal. Her eyes throw me a slow once over, waist to hairline, roots to flower, then back to roots.

Franny Dahler, Ms. Strawberry, leaves my office grinning like a circus clown.

Think she noticed my enthusiasm?

I have more crap paperwork to sign than a U.S. Army supply sergeant. It's eight o'clock before I close up Shore Securities for the weekend and begin to dream of Luis's place and Umberto's green-chili burritos.

A motion sensor illuminates the back parking lot as I walk to my Camry, but the neighboring businesses are closed, and a solid ring of darkness encircles the well-lighted parking area.

Like a spotlighted performer, my skin tingles with the sensation of being watched.

TWENTY-TWO

Max squeezes into the shotgun seat of Jerry's rumbling new silver Corvette. Max's knees stretch the dashboard. His right shoulder bends the door glass. He feels like stick of gum in a shiny metal wrapper.

Max contorts his upper body to reach the window button, uses his hand to tug on his left leg, squashing his nuts to make room for Jerry to work the Corvette's floor-mounted gear shift.

"Let's steal a car quick," Max says. "A big one."

Jerry guns the loud V-8 engine, racing the car's four-hundred horsepower like a NASCAR driver. Or a kid with a new toy. Max knows Jerry four years now and each one is the same. Fast cars and faster women. Only thing new is fancier suits and big diamond earring Jerry wears since he started playing golf with ex-pro football players.

"You see something with New York plates, holler," Jerry says. "Otherwise, I know a good spot on the other side of the tunnel."

Max points with his left hand, his index finger touching the Corvette's windshield. "Pull into bus lot one mile ahead, right by entrance to Parkway. Many New York cars park there, take the bus to Atlantic City casinos."

"Yeah? All right, let's try it. Look for a Lincoln Town Car, or a Caddy, some snazzy wheels. I heard the chef at this place we're going to cooks for gourmets at the James Beard House."

Max grunts.

"What's the matter?"Jerry says.

Jerry points the Corvette's shiny silver nose toward the Garden State Parkway. Road rushes past like black river of individual rocks, the sports car so close to the ground. A cold wind stings Max's face.

"Come on, Max. I know you. What's the matter?"

"We should hide, wait for mark in his bedroom," Max says.

"The boss's way is better."

"No mistakes when I catch mark by surprise," Max says.

Jerry glances at him. "What the hell are you worried about? Not that bartender's lucky kick?"

Max breathes deeply. "Bartender was quick like cat. Only a little lucky."

"Nothing like that ever happened before. A freakin' fluke's what that was."

Maybe Jerry is right. "Is true Max only get knocked down twice in whole life."

Jerry brakes at a red light, hits the right turn signal. Click-click. Click-click. The bus parking lot is just across the street. Max will be much happier in bigger car. So will Max's nuts.

"I bet the other time was an elephant," Jerry says.

Max says nothing. Elephants are usually nice. It was a big cat that brought Max to his knees. A mean smelly lion named Victor.

TWENTY-THREE

At the two-gas-station corner of Broad Street and Willow, a black or midnight-blue new Lincoln Town Car matches my turn. When I straighten out and accelerate, the Lincoln's wide headlights perfectly mimic my Camry's modest speed, holding exactly half-a-block back. Like I was towing the puppy.

We're traveling north on Highway 35, but I'm guessing my Friday evening just turned south.

Figures I'm being followed. In two weeks time, Austin Carr has seen two lifetimes worth of threatened financial ruin, fights, beatings, fires, assaults, and murder. Not to mention interrogations, accusations, and obfuscation. I've been betrayed, befuddled, and bewildered. Of course I'm being followed.

I slide the Toyota over a lane and lock the doors. For the umpteenth time since Mr. Vick sailed for Tuscany and Walter sold my friendship for half a million dollars, I ask myself how violence and disaster so easily enter my life. Potential injury or death, a nonexistent love life, and looming bankruptcy stalk my good humor like a trio of vultures.

Just before the next intersection, I flip the wheel hard left, ducking in front of oncoming traffic and bouncing the Camry into a Burger King. A triple-beef, triple cheese sounds good. My libido needs to substitute.

All four of the Camry's wheels go into a slide, but I swerve and pump the gas pedal just in time, carefully avoiding the eight-foot plastic, TV-commercial famous King character who serves as menu to the drive-thru line.

Think this U.S.-built, Japanese car with Mexican and Chinese parts would have wiped off that happy bastard's frozen smile?

In my mirror, I see the Lincoln Town Car cruise past the second and final Burger King entrance. I don't get even a peek at the driver or passengers, thanks to his tinted windows.

I skulk in BK's back lot five or six minutes. No sign of the Lincoln. I should have ordered a Coke and that triple-triple while I sailed past the King. Maybe a shake and an order of fries.

Two parked cars leave, and I spot an alley. Should I run for it? Seems like the natural thing to do. For me, anyway. I did the peyote thing with a Native American friend once, as a kid, and discovered through trial and hallucination that my animal spirit guide is a horse. Nervous, with extra-long legs for the get-out-of-here giddy-up.

I yank off a nasty, rubber-burning K-turn in front of an angry mom and two wide-eyed kids in a minivan, hit the unmarked back exit sliding left, doubling back toward Branchtown. Austin Carr is The Transporter.

Must be garbage day tomorrow. Overflowing tin and plastic trash cans litter the dark alley on both sides. Instead of a palomino stallion, I feel like a bowling ball curling down a waxed lane. The Camry racks up two spares and a strike. Trash cans are flying.

I'm twenty-five feet from the next side street when a black shadow fills the alley. I hit the brakes too late, skidding to a bump-stop against the black or midnight blue Lincoln Town Car's rear door. In the same thumping moment, the Camry's steering wheel explodes and an air bag punches my face.

By the time I get the giant nylon marshmallow out of my mouth and fight my way outside, I'm standing beside the one and only Tony Farascio. He's wearing his usual golf magazine apparel, a full-boat grin on his George Clooney lips. His sausage of a thumb points toward the Lincoln that's been following me.

The shotgun-side window slides down. Gina waves.

TWENTY-FOUR

I'm slowly adapting to my new environment: Black Ford Motor Company leather. Buffed silver and polished walnut trim. Riding with the King and Queen of the Brooklyn mafia's spring prom.

Last time I saw Gina she wanted to shoot her husband with some kind of bazooka-size handgun. Now the two of them are all kissy-kissy, Tony's knockout wife looking extra sexy in a silky black dress.

"Hungry?" Gina says.

Like she can't tell. "I'll let you know when my stomach grows back."

"Did we scare you?" she says.

"Not more than Boris Karloff when I was six."

Tony laughs. Not Gina. She hasn't smiled at me since I climbed in behind them. I'm in the back seat of the Farascio's Lincoln. The air tastes of leather and perfume, or maybe it's Tony's after-shave. On the radio, Frank Sinatra sings "Summer Wind."

"We were having a little fun, sunshine," Tony says to me. "Don't worry about your car. I'll take care of the towing...everything."

"What the hell happened at the hotel, Tony?"

"You got forty-five minutes to work up an appetite," he says. "Maybe longer if the tunnel's choked up. You're eating at the best Italian restaurant in Little Italy."

Oh, boy. Comfort food. "Instead of dinner, how about discussing you disappearing with Bluefish's hundred grand? Maybe a line or two about Talbot turning up dead? What the hell happened?"

The Farascios trade glances.

"Wait 'til you taste the baked mac," Gina says.

Hanging twine-covered wine bottles camouflage three short walls of the narrow, one-room restaurant. A single glass window faces Mulberry Street. A tiny bar and fourteen white-linen tables fill the boxcar like space. Me and the Farascios take up two, Tony needing a table all by himself.

Green bell pepper-shaped wall lamps provide the only inside light. Sinatra is playing in here, too. Some Doris Day love song from the early sixties I don't even want to remember the name of. Truth is, I'm a bit dizzy. Can't shake this time-warp feel. It's either a Sinatra overload, or maybe it's because Tony just told me to "forget about" Bluefish and the money, "not to worry 'bout nuttin'."

"Bluefish will back off me and Luis just because you tell him to?" I say.

"Ab-so-fucking-lutely," Tony says. "And he'll eat the one-hundred gees I took from him, too. The war's over. It's already been explained to Bluefish."

I'm far from expert on mob organizational matters, but I suppose it's logical that a New York mafia family would hold sway over a bookie from Branchtown, New Jersey. Maybe Tony can have Bluefish and The Creeper called off. Mr. Vick certainly gave me Tony's number for a reason.

I hope Mr. Vick didn't know about this mob trouble before he left for Tuscany. I'd have to kill him when he gets back.

"But what about Talbot?" I say. "Did you go to her room? Did you see her?"

"Sure," Tony says. "She's an old friend. I gave her a taste of Bluefish's cash, explained about me and Vick, and now everything's cool. No more co-mingling. She was okay when I left her."

Gina's fist goes for her husband's face like a firecracker. But Tony's quicker. He catches her wrist, Gina's white knuckles six inches from contact.

"Bastard!"

"Not here," he says. "Please."

Gina screaming, "You gave her a taste, all right, didn't you, asshole? A taste of your prick."

Tony's fingers turn white around Gina's wrist. She winces from the pain. Her eyes flash submission. Her lips press together in forced silence.

Gosh I'm glad I came to dinner with the Farascios.

TWENTY-FIVE

Tony saying to me, "What're you lookin at?"

"Nothing."

Not a lie actually because Anthony Farascio's question should have been, what's looking at us. Gina in particular. Not that I'm about to tell Tony that two other very rough-looking gentlemen are ogling his wife. This joint being the Farascio's turf, I figure Gina's husband would exhibit few qualms initiating combat over her honor. I'm afraid on Mulberry Street this means we could all die in a haze of armor-piercing bullets.

Personally, I'd rather sample the baked macaroni, get back to Jersey.

"Don't brush me off," Tony says. "Somebody checking us out?"

Damn. Here it is again, that special Austin Carr moment when I know what I am about to say will produce inevitable and disastrous repercussions. Nevertheless, I will make my little speech because I'm a blabbermouth who craves the sound of his own voice.

"Two guys came in a minute ago, sat behind you," I say. "Seems like they might know you...and Gina."

Boy, I wish I'd kept my mouth shut. When am I going to learn? This Gift of Gab is becoming a major and serious handicap. Wonder if I could get one of those special license plates with the embossed wheelchair?

Tony spins to check out the new customers.

Gina's gaze has been avoiding mine all night. Now her dark eyes fix on me, a hard angry glare. She tosses a chunk of bread at my chest. She was about to dip it into a dish of green olive oil.

Guess she thinks I'm a blabbermouth, too.

Tony's German Shepherd eyes drift back to me and Gina. "Wise guys," he says. "The one with the shrimp lips is named Jimmy something. I know the other one, too." He focuses on Gina. "They're both part of Nunzio's crew."

Gina frowns. "What are they doing here?"

"I don't know," Tony says. "Think I have to ask 'em."

Over Tony's shoulder, movement draws my gaze. "You don't have to," I say. "They're coming over."

Sinatra is singing "New York, New York" now, his big studio orchestra filling cracks in the little restaurant's stucco walls like slick grout. Wine bottles rattle. The smell of tomato sauce hovers like fog.

Tony stares at my nose, then over my shoulder. "Which one you want?"

"They don't look like they're going to start anything," I say. "Seems like they just want to say hello."

"I'm not talking about the two guys behind me," Tony says. "I'm talking about the two behind you."

My head snaps. The Creeper and his friend with a diamond earring are headed our way.

Gina saying, "This would be a great time to show these people your gun, Tony."

"I left it in the Town Car," he says.

"Perfect," I say. "In case we need it later."

The one Tony calls Shrimp Lips stops closest to Gina. His lips really do look like boiled crustacean. Pink with blistered white stripes. Bet he's a lousy kisser. He says to Gina, "Hiya, Sugar. Want to dance?"

Gina makes a show of her unsuccessful search for a dance floor. "Where?" she says. "On the table?"

Shrimp Lips focuses on Gina's cleavage. Slow and deliberate, leering and insulting. "Honey, with that set of tits, I'd be happy if we just wiggled around right—"

My jaw falls off.

Tony's right fist leads his shoulder and hips out of his seat. His knuckles flash against Shrimp Lips's gooey mouth. The sound of breaking teeth cracks the air like a whip.

Gina's molester tumbles into the neighboring table. Men yell. Women scream. Plates, glasses, and silverware crash and break.

Shrimp Lips grabs a tablecloth on the way down. More dishes

and glasses bust on the floor.

Gina and two other women scream.

It's like watching one of Sam Peckinpaw's slow-motion fight scenes. Everyone in the restaurant was watching. Now they're fighting. Every single face distorts with anger and frustration. Their grunts and groans erupt around the room like a series of steam jets.

A thick arm encircles my neck, choking off my air. Sinatra's voice soars to a big finish.

New York, New York, my ass.

Might have blacked out for a second there. I guess it's Shrimp Lips's partner choking me. Don't know for certain because I can't see behind me, and even if I could, I probably couldn't because my eyes are bulging halfway out of their sockets.

If that makes any sense. Maybe the lack of oxygen is affecting my cognitive abilities. I wish somebody would turn off Sinatra before he starts "My Way."

A fist hits me in the mouth. Whoa. The python around my neck rips over my ears as I fall against and onto an exceptionally sturdy wooden chair. Before my feet find solid ground, a giant wild beast compresses my chest into wallboard.

Must be a moose or a grizzly bear pushing against me. Destroying my urban illusion of being in control of nature.

No. Wait. It's human. Almost.

The Creeper.

Notice I said "destroying" urban illusions, not "decimating?" TV newscasters and movie scriptwriters think the words are interchangeable, and they eventually will be, of course, thanks to never-ending misuse.

But for now, and the last five-hundred years anyway, decimate means to reduce by ten percent. It's the only thing I learned in high school Latin class. It's what Caesar used to do to his troops when food ran low. Centurions would count off every tenth man and kill him. A scene of slaughter, oh yeah, but hardly the same as destroy. Ninety percent survived a decimation.

A shrieking lizard-brain alarm goes off when I realize what I've been thinking about. I'm definitely running short of air. Playing *Jeopardy* while my oxygen depletes. Caesar and his Centurions.

I twist my face right, gasp a mouthful of air, then throw my shoulders to the left. I successfully almost break my neck.

Fists punch my face. My head gets smacked against the floor. I hear a voice in my head begin to hum. Gina's screams become a distant wailing.

The buzz in my head grows louder and louder until it's a spinning circle of smoky black sleep. The dark tornado sucks me inside.

TWENTY-SIX

"Come on, get up."

The familiar, thickly accented voice cancels a nightmare about having my head crushed. Is that Mama Bones? What is she doing here? Or, more to the point, where the hell am I?

My head's full of blood and mucous, ready to split like an overripe olive. My nose feels like a wad of prosciutto. Oh, yeah. Now I remember. I'm at the best little Italian restaurant in Little Italy. The joint right off Mulberry Street where three humans and The Creeper beat up one unlucky table of guests before the pasta's served. Keeps the other customers in line.

I roll to my hands and knees, let Mama Bones's sturdy two-handed grip tow me onto my feet. Whoa. Mr. Vick's mother owns major grasping and pulling forearms. Like Caterpillar back-hoes. Mama Bones must fill out a lot of phony bingo cards.

Two young men I remember from Mr. Vick's sailing-away party in Atlantic Highlands stand watchfully behind Mama Bones. Dark-haired, dark-eyed. Wearing black chinos, black Nikes, and black T-shirts. Mr. Trim and Mr. Fit.

What's up with them?

"No time to answer questions," Mama Bones says. "This is Thomas, this one Gianni."

Wonder if there's anything to Mr. Vick's claim his mother actually reads minds? Nah. It's obvious I would have a question, right?

Mama Bones squats her ample butt down beside Gina and touches the younger woman's shoulder. Her hand rubs Gina's back. It's a side of Mr. Vick's mother I've never witnessed before. Almost

84

warm. Like five-minute-old toast.

"We gotta go, honey," Mama Bones says.

Gina's hands and gaze won't leave Tony's face, the dark-haired beauty no longer Queen of Anything, just a shocked and frightened woman. Kind of the way I felt when The Creeper hauled me and Ryan about the Locust Tree Inn dining room with one arm around each of us like we were broken lamps.

"Tony's hurt," Gina says. "We have to get help."

Mama Bones leans across Gina and touches Tony's neck. Her fingers don't stay in contact more than three or four seconds. "We take him to hospital," Mama says. She waves for Thomas and Gianni to lift him.

"Come on. Get up," she says to Gina.

"I hear a siren," Gina says. "I should stay and tell the police."

Mama shakes her head. "At'sa no good idea, Angelina. This Brooklyn. If cops keep you overnight, Tony's people have you killed in jail."

"Tony's people? Why would they hurt me?"

Just what I was going to ask. We have a lot in common, Gina and me.

"Who you think ordered this, huh?"Mama Bones says. "You think Bluefish send Jersey people to Brooklyn without permission?"

Gina's crying. Between sniffs, she says, "Nunzio?"

Mama Bones leads our hurried, shuffling troop through a suddenly empty kitchen. Gee, where did the staff go? The chefs and chefettes are hiding.

Or maybe it's that over-blended, caustic smell of roasting lamb shanks, grilled liver, sautéed fish, and burned broccoli that drove them away. I know I could use some fresh air.

Outside, in an alley busy with delivery vans and trucks, Gina first tumbles in behind the driver's seat of a very clean white Cadillac Escalade. But when Gianni and Thomas stretch Tony out in the extended trunk, Gina changes her mind, wants to ride in back with her husband.

Gina screams when she crawls up close beside him. Uh, oh.

Mama Bones grips my arm. "Her husband is dead," she says. "That animal Max break Tony's neck."

TWENTY-SEVEN

Travel directly to Manhattan after your flight into Newark-Liberty International Airport and the New Jersey you'll remember involves refineries, garbage, and rust. Very American, of course. But decidedly unappealing.

To snap another shot of Jersey, drive south on the Turnpike, then down the Garden State Parkway half an hour, watch the scenery transform into forests of maple, pine, and oak. Rivers and salt-water sloughs; farms with horses and barns. Central New Jersey's rural suburbs best anything in Connecticut or Massachusetts.

Of course, another thirty minutes south on the Parkway and you're in New Jersey's Pine Barrens, a desert-like, endless brush of stunted, twisted, yellowed evergreen scrub that makes the night drive from L.A. to Las Vegas look scenic.

"Where are we going?" I say.

"Somewhere Bluefish no look for you."

Besides the accent, Mama Bones's language and tone also carry a certain confidence I wish I could share. When Gina saw Tony was dead, and went off like a hotel smoke detector, it was Mama Bones who brought Gina back with a small smack and a quickly mumbled shaman's spell. The old woman's bag of tricks definitely carries mojo. But I just witnessed a murder, and I can identify at least three of the four murderers. If I'm Bluefish, I not only look under every rock for Austin Carr, I station a man there.

Gianni's driving the Escalade. Thomas rides shotgun. Mama Bones, a nonverbal Gina, and yours truly stack the next row. Tony's still in the back. Hard to believe the guy with German Shepherd eyes wound up dead while searching for a good plate of baked mac.

"If Bluefish's people wanted Gina dead, why didn't they kill her tonight?" I say.

"Their orders were to kill just Tony," Mama Bones says. "Gina was supposed to get a phone call and be out of restaurant. No witness. But now, when Bluefish find out you and Gina were there to see his men kill Tony, he will sure try to kill both of you."

Gina leans against me, her body loose from exhaustion. Despite all that's happened, my shock over Tony's murder, Gina's weight warms me in places I shouldn't be getting warm. Unbelievable. It's rare, I admit, but sometimes even Austin Carr can show couth.

"How do you know all this, Mama Bones?" I say.

Mama Bones leans forward to touch Gianni's shoulder. "Is next exit."

It's not an easy movement to pick up on, the dark-haired, black-shirted young man presenting only minimum outlines, but Gianni nods.

"How you think I know, smarty pants?" Mama Bones says. "Maybe me and Bluefish in the same business, you think? Maybe I work for Bluefish?"

"And he told you they were planning to kill—"

"Bluefish tell me nothing," she says.

Gianni guides the Escalade off the Parkway. We roll through a stop sign at the end of the short off ramp, turn right onto a ribbon of blacktop running into the pine forest. A full-grown deer bounds into the SUV's headlights, and then is gone. Planets stare and stars blink at us from a narrow strip of sky between the trees.

"But you heard what was going to happen," I say, "and tried to help Vick's friend Tony?"

The SUV's tires hum against my feet through the floorboard. Another deer watches us from the tree line, this one's eyes glowing neon yellow. Or do these night-vision lenses belong to some other kind of animal? A night hunter, perhaps. Sharp beaks, or a mouth with fangs.

"I mean, I know you didn't come to save me," I say.

Mama, Gianni, and Thomas laugh on cue like a warmed-up TV taping audience. Johnny Carson never had a crowd so well prepped. Maybe I'm funnier than Groucho Marx, but I don't think so.

Gina's fingers touch my arm. "Mama Bones came for me," she says. "She's my aunt. My mother's sister. I'm named after her."

Angelina. Right. I knew that.

TWENTY-EIGHT

Mama Bones keys the entrance. The scrub-pine forest grows within twenty feet of the roofed, plank-board porch that encircles the two-story hunting lodge we're about to enter. Behind us, a dirt clearing offers space for three dump trucks, two school buses, and a Boeing 747 beside the white Escalade.

An owl hoots. The Jersey night air smells of dry pine needles and a distant charcoal campfire. I hope Thomas or Gianni brought marshmallows.

Inside, Mama Bones flips a light switch. Whoa. A forty-by-forty-foot hotel lobby greets my eyes—a dozen leather lounge chairs, overstuffed sofas, green felt card tables, brass lamps, and two televisions. Pine floors. Pine walls. With animal heads.

"Some joint," I say.

"Don't get comfortable," Mama Bones says. "You only safe here a day or two."

"Then what?"

She shrugs. "Is up to you. I bring you here, make you safe for a while because you with Gina. Rest of your life is up to you."

Nice. Mama Bones would make a great stockbroker. Better yet, a bond trader. "You're leaving me here all alone?"

Mama Bones shakes her head. "Gianni give you his bug-out bag."

"Oh boy. Whatever the hell that is. What about Gina?"

"I take her somewhere else."

I sigh. Mama Bones has that conversation-over tone in her voice, not to mention the upper hand. Gina's her family. Guess I'm lucky to be alive, actually. But I'll have to be even luckier to stay above ground. Every time I think my situation can't get worse, it does. At least Ryan and Beth are safe.

"Bedroom upstairs," Mama Bones says.

I glance toward the stairway. The hand-carved log railing and banister is a sculpture. Twisted tree branches, bull horns, cowboys, and horse heads grow from the wood like living images of the Wild West.

"Who owns this place?"

"Bluefish," Mama Bones says. "Me and Thomas figure it's last place he look."

Gina steps out of the Escalade to hug me. It's a halfhearted embrace, the dark-haired widow dabbing back tears with a tissue.

Over my shoulder, she says, "Did you tell him everything, Mama Bones?"

"He knows plenty," Mama Bones says.

"Mama? We discussed this," Gina says. "Austin needs to know the story on Anne Marie. To save Shore Securities...for himself, yes, but also for your son and your granddaughter Carmela."

Mama Bones shifts her gaze to mine. Like she's trying to decide if she wants to turn me into a frog. Whoa. Why did I think that, for crissakes? Who put that in my mind? Think happy thoughts, Austin. Happy thoughts.

"If you don't, I will," Gina says.

Mama Bones grunts. "Anne Marie Talbot is notta just any accountant for the A.A.S.D. She do favors all the time for Bluefish and others before him. This time, she is working for Bluefish. She is supposed to put squeeze on you, help Bluefish take over Shore Securities."

The owl hoots again. A gust of night air hisses at me through pine needles. There's more. There has to be.

"And..."Gina says.

"And that's why my son Vittorio go to Italy, leave you in charge of Shore," Mama Bones says. "He knows Rags can't pay, that Bluefish come after him because he introduce Rags, vouch for him. Plus my little Vittorio figures this A.A.S.D. investigation is rigged against him."

My jaw drops. "Mr. Vick left me to take the heat? He was

90

willing to risk my family's lives, not his?"

Mama Bones nods.

That son-of-a-bitch. I'm going to drive a full set of Wilson irons up his spaghetti-eating ass. Plus the bag and cart.

But below the anger, another more logical jewel of thought shines to the top. "Do you know who killed Anne Marie?" I say.

Mama Bones glances at Gina. Mrs. Farascio nods permission.

"Brooklyn believe Tony did it for the hundred-thousand," Mama Bones says. "That's what Bluefish tell them, anyway. He say he had video recording, then lost DVD to cops. Brooklyn guys believe him, say okay to hit Tony."

"Nunzio's been jealous of Tony for years," Gina says.

"Where did Bluefish get a video of Talbot's murder?" I say.

"I don't know," Mama Bones says. "Is only rumor I hear."

"But you don't think Tony really did it?"

She looks at Gina. "No."

Why do I feel her answer might be different if Tony's wife wasn't here? Wasn't it Mama Bones who told me Tony was "abada-bada man?"

TWENTY-NINE

I am so pissed at Mr. Vick, I can't sleep. That son-of-a-bitch con man might as well have stenciled bulls-eyes on my children's backs.

Plus, I have to question my choice of business partners. First Walter, now Mr. Vick. And that's not even mentioning wacky Rags. I couldn't have done any worse choosing business associates if I'd used the Seaside County criminal detention center as a source pool.

Hard to believe my golfing-jerk-buddy boss, Vick Bonacelli, would do this. Except, thinking semi-objectively for unbroken hours, enough moonlight to see only gray through Bluefish's second-story window, I figure putting my family up as a target must have been the only way Mr. Vick could think of to protect his children.

Not that I forgive the dick-wad.

My body heaves and pitches, my molars grind all night, imagining what I'm going to do next time I see him. Scream in his face? Punch his classic Roman nose? Use a Barry Bonds, thirty-four-ounce baseball bat to adjust the worst golf swing in Seaside County?

Just before dawn, I'm glad for the Vick-hating insomnia. As the north eastern New Jersey sky finally lightens to blue-steel in the bedroom window, the crunch of automobile tires on dirt announces someone's arrival.

The approaching tire-sounds roll me off Bluefish's California king. I know Branchtown's Godfather Wannabe sleeps here because, on a plaque above this swimming pool-size feather-soft bed, a twenty-three pound specimen of his namesake fish smiles back at me.

I slept—no, rested—on top of the blue satin bedcovers because I didn't want to worry how clean his sheets were, what dried body fluids or particulate remnants I might be touching. Yuk. I can't believe I even thought of that.

Two long strides put me at the window. This is the only bedroom with a view of the driveway and front-door parking area.

Crows squawk somewhere close as I carefully slide back the curtain. A Lincoln Town Car skids to a soil-pushing stop. The driver-door pops open. Creeper squeezes out like toothpaste.

Oh, joy. The sight of him kicks my heart rate. My legs want to flee down the stairs, race out the back, run through the forest till I'm safe and hidden.

Instead, I remain frozen by the window while Creeper thunders up the steps and rattles keys, unlocking the split-log front door. Doesn't he have to huff and puff or something? Blow my house down?

The Creeper's sure making a lot of noise, though. Maybe that means he doesn't know I'm here.

THIRTY

Soon as he sees the complicated electronic controls—so many dials, switches, and gauges—Max wishes he made Jerry come with him. Only thing Max knows about electronics is on/off switches. Plus, English is most hardest language for Max to read. What if he misses an important warning, an instruction? What if, in trying to use this smoker, Max burns down Bluefish's hunting lodge?

Screw it. Like Jerry always says. All Max have to do is make heat, not cook the meat. Ha-ha.

Max locates what he hopes is the main on/off switch, and then the digital control with a read-out for recommended temperatures. His thick forefinger finds and pokes the up arrow on a control switch, and presto, a red number appears. Two-hundred degrees should be plenty. Today's mark is already half-dead.

Bluefish's meat smoker is big enough to hold two whole deer, one on each rack. But clearly Max's job will be easier if he makes the space as large as possible. The mark may come to life when he sees where Max wants to put him.

Max slides out the chrome rack and sets the table-sized grill on the floor, leaning it against the basement wall. The clink of metal hitting cold cement echoes in the nearly barren room. He leaves the smoker door open when he goes outside to get the mark.

Max shuffles through the lodge's big living room, across the porch, and then down the front steps to the Lincoln Town Car. A pink sky shows where the east wind lives. The air smells of coming rain and lightning.

God is about to get pissy.

From the Lincoln's trunk, Max lifts the mark off the spare tire and onto his shoulders. Though limp now, the young man fought hard earlier. A tough and loyal soldier, this man didn't make a sound or give up one piece of information when Jerry cut him.

But this mark not so tough and loyal Bluefish's smoker won't make him talk. Fire and heat make strong people speak for thousands and thousands of years.

Even lions make noise when fire come. Cry like babies.

THIRTY-ONE

I scramble for the bedroom window again when I hear Creeper's weight stretch the porch boards. Through dusty glass, I watch Creeper shuffle down the front steps, the big man's arms and hips maintaining a bouncy rhythm all the way to the Lincoln Town Car. Looks like he might be whistling.

Gee, how nice Creeper's in such a happy mood. Maybe Bluefish wants him to strangle somebody.

Creeper opens the Lincoln's trunk. I have a good angle because of where he parked, and I can see directly...whoa...there's a man inside, apparently dead, or at least dead drunk. Looks like it might be Gianni or Thomas. Whichever, Mama Bones's sidekick lifts his head, jerks his eyes open while he's bouncing on Creeper's shoulders.

Glad he's not dead. But this means I have to do something. Doesn't it? Mama Bones and those two men—Mr. Trim and Mr. Fit—pulled my ass out of a nasty spot a few hours ago. I can't run away from their trouble.

Can I?

Well, I could. A lot of stock jockeys I know would duck for an exit. And like I said before I jumped on Rags over a week ago, I'm no hero. I have no desire to test myself against Creeper. Are you kidding? It's just that...well, if Creeper has captured Gianni or Thomas, whichever, what does that say about the present physical condition of lovely Gina Farascio and my charge, Mama Bones?

In particular, I keep thinking about Gina.

Although maybe right now isn't the best time. My breath comes in short shallow gasps. My heart's clunking like a broken electric fan.

I unzip Gianni's bug-out bag, a camouflage-painted canvas

carryall of the size soccer-goalies bring to games. Inside there's a red climbing rope with clips and fittings and hooks, a pair of new blue jeans, a wool shirt, a green down jacket, a cell phone, sixty bucks cash, dry matches, a compass, eight protein bars, a waterproof tarp, a twelve-inch K-Bar hunting knife, water bottles, and...oh, my...a snub-nose Smith & Wesson thirty-eight.

Fully loaded.

With an extra box of bullets.

I'm tiptoeing down the lodge's basement steps when someone—I assume Gianni or Thomas—screams. The sound pokes my gut like one of Umberto's rare-but-deadly over-spiced burritos.

The narrow, dank stairway feels like a mine shaft, the rock smooth and gray. I travel down to the basement one careful step at a time, the Smith & Wesson held in front of me like an airline vomit bag.

There was nothing in my Series Seven stockbroker's study guide to indicate the correct grip for revolvers, but I do my best at the bottom of the steps. I imagine Detective Sipowicz, deploy the two-handed, eye-level position.

I read in the newspaper once that real cops think Sipowicz is right-on aces.

What I see in Bluefish's cement basement rattles my already less-than-Sipowiczian courage, however. Hell, who am I kidding? I damn near pee my pants. Creeper has Gianni—I recognize the hairline now—hoisted in the air, Gianni's bare feet stuck inside some kind of oven. At the bottom of the huge aluminum appliance, directly beneath Gianni's tootsies, an electric element glows red hot.

"Get him out of there," I say.

Creeper gazes at my revolver like it's a fish taco. That is, strange.

Gianni screams.

I fire at Creeper's knees.

The noise of the gunshot slams my brain. The explosion seems to bounce around the cement room like a foul ball in empty seats, finally rolling to a stop. My vision blurs, and my sinuses vibrate like a church bell.

Creeper doesn't blink at the noise. His gaze slowly drops toward his feet, then focuses at the new white chip in the basement's cement floor.

Can't believe I missed. Creeper's knees are as big as steamer trunks.

Gianni's screams again reach my battered eardrums. I step closer and raise the weapon to target Creeper's nose. Don't remember seeing Sipowicz do this, but it feels right. My finger pressures the trigger. Funny, but I don't think killing this man would bother me much. Creeper's the kind of monster who could have killed my children the other night without a qualm.

The big man must read my mind because he pulls Gianni's feet from the oven thingy. It doesn't look like an oven, really. I resist an urge to shoot anyway. Creeper's going to kill you if you don't kill him, a voice whispers. Think of it in terms of Beth and Ryan's future.

Instead, I use the Smith & Wesson to wave Creeper away from the aluminum appliance. What would I do without TV and the movies? First the two-handed grip, now the gun as casual directional aide. Who needs firearm lessons?

When Creeper's tucked away where he can't reach me, I tell him to put Gianni down and walk backward toward the big cooking machine.

"Is smoker," Creeper says. Grinning at me with ugly teeth. Still holding Gianni across his shoulders like a recently bagged wild animal.

"I don't care if it's a tanning lamp," I say. "Put him down—carefully—and walk over beside the smoker. Snuggle up. This thirty-eight won't blow your head off, but you won't hear the shot either."

Creeper lets Gianni's slide off his shoulders and lays him out gently on the bare cement floor. Silence hasn't returned to the basement air just yet. My first gunshot still plays like the last chord of a rock anthem.

When Creeper slides over by the smoker, I use Gianni's hunting knife from the bug-out bag to cut the duct tape binding his wrists and knees.

"You okay?" I say.

Gianni groans, says two or three words I can't make out. His bare feet are black on the bottom with white blisters bubbling like bacon on the scarlet insteps. My stomach tells me to forget about breakfast.

From behind and above a voice says, "Put down the gun,

98

Austin."

THIRTY-TWO

My heart skips two beats while my brain accepts one disturbing image: Gianni's brother Thomas and a Vin Diesel Wannabe fill the basement stairway, both of them pointing assault rifles at me.

Reminds me of the last time new-issue stocks were hot. Clients get angry when you can't get them shares they know are going to triple. One has yet to show up with an assault rifle, but I think it's only a matter of time.

"I'm on your side," I say. I'm talking to Gianni, but my gaze stays on Creeper. A little voice tells me my life depends on it.

"For the moment we're on the same side," Thomas says. "So do your new pal a favor and put the gun down."

The basement floor chills my knuckles as I lay the Smith & Wesson beside Gianni's shoulder. The sound clicks too loudly in the still basement air. Maybe I'm hyperventilating. My stomach says I definitely won't be eating for a week.

Under the artful direction of Thomas, his tattooed, shaved-head sidekick, and their straight-from-Baghdad assault rifles, Creeper and I load Gianni into the back of the same white Escalade I rode in last night. Hope Gianni's story turns out happier than Tony's. Now that I think about it, guess Gianni's already doing better.

The closeness of Creeper's mountainous mass keeps my nerves on a sharp blade. It's like walking beside a leashed and trained grizzly bear. Everything's cool—as long as he doesn't change his mind about closely monitored captivity.

Thomas motions with the muzzle of his automatic rifle for

Creeper to move away, toward the lodge's pine board porch. Creeper obeys, I'm sure because his mother raised him to be polite, and perhaps also because Thomas's weapon can deliver large-caliber bullets like water through a hose.

I figure I'm in. Thomas didn't send me over to the steps. But when I reach for the Caddy's door handle, Thomas's bald friend stiff-arms my chest.

"You're not coming," Thomas says.

"You're leaving me here with Creeper?"

"Ha. Good name for him. And yeah, you stay because we've had enough of this fight. I want Max to know it. I want him to tell Bluefish."

That doesn't sound like good news. For me, anyway. And my stomach was just returning to normal. Wonder if that bug-out bag has any Alka-Seltzer?

"You hear that, Max?" Thomas says. He turns to face Bluefish's henchman. "I'm taking my brother back, that's all. I don't care what you did to him. This little war is over now. You can have Carr as a peace offering."

My head does a full-boat neck swivel, a slow search for escape routes. Hmm. Too bad I can't fly. Looks like this stockbroker will soon be high-tailing it into the woods.

"Don't worry," Thomas says to me. "You've got Bluefish's Town Car there, plus my brother's bug-out bag. When I leave, I'll toss your gun back."

I feel so much better.

"Or at least," Thomas says, "I'll toss it closest to you."

Does knowing someone's planning to kill you give you license to kill that person first? Aiming the Smith & Wesson at Creeper's garage door of a chest, I decide yes, it probably does. But I'm still not going to shoot him.

Not yet, anyway.

"Give me the keys to the Lincoln," I say.

Thomas and his hairless friend left fifteen seconds ago. I can still hear the car's engine. The film of dust the tires kicked up just now floats into the space between me and Creeper. The fog of war. Think maybe I'm being a little dramatic?

Luckily, I did in fact beat Creeper to the gun. Despite enjoying a good ball bust, Thomas must have appreciated my interest in Gianni. I did make Creeper take Gianni's feet out of the smoker.

I walk closer, less than eight-feet away from this huge monster of a man who threatened my children. Slowly, I aim the gun at Creeper's nose. This worked before. I like precedent.

"Only one more time I say this, Max. Give me the keys."

Creeper grins. His teeth look like a recently thinned forest. Lots of dark empty spaces and broken, snapped-off stumps.

I pressure the trigger.

Creeper digs into his pocket, eases out a baseball-size gob of brass and chrome keys. His huge fingers work on the tiny pieces of metal like a silversmith, quickly separating a gold-colored one.

Creeper knows I'm not bluffing.

The big man shows me the gold key he's removed from the key chain, pointing at the logo so I know it's for a Ford product, then stuffs the puppy in his mouth and swallows.

Ouch.

Bastard's not as dumb as those teeth make him look. What I mean, Creeper can tell by looking at me I won't shoot him unless I absolutely have to. But how does a guy learn to trust instincts like that? Bigger than ballsy, if you ask me. Like a guy who'd wrestle two bears at the same time.

"You going to shoot me?" Creeper says.

God, I hate that grin on his face.

But...it does seem like I'm out of options. Waiting around for Creeper to pass the key through his system sure isn't an alternative I'd like to explore. Can you imagine what his...?

"Okay, smart ass," I say. "I'm going to disappear into these woods. If I hear you following me, I'll stop, hide, and shoot you on sight."

Creeper's grin stretches into a long, twisted smile. It's an ugly thing, like the winner of a most-frightening jack-o-lantern contest. Halloween eyes and dagger teeth from Hell.

The look on him sucks my breath away.

Makes me wonder if a bullet to the brain would even kill him.

THIRTY-THREE

I stumble on an embedded pine cone and knock my shoulder against the denuded limb of an otherwise-yellowish evergreen. Must be two-hundred billion bad-ass ugly trees in New Jersey's Pine Barrens. And half of them are staring back at me, blocking my course. I feel like a tick fighting his way through dog hair.

My progress is slow and increasingly less steady through, around, and under these nasty scrub pine trees. Underline slow. Adding to my inevitable immobility, Gianni's bug-out bag tows behind me like a dead horse.

Although there is a lot of good shit in here.

Checking the enclosed compass, for instance, I know I'm hiking due east. This is strategically important because I can't negotiate two steps without tripping over a cone, make two yards without ducking under a snapped limb. I've suffered tougher getting a bathroom stall at Giant Stadium, true, but keeping my direction would be impossible for this backwoods tenderfoot were it not for Gianni's unusual compass.

Inside a black plastic hexagon, a bubble lens magnifies a tightly bunched field of art—the N, S, E and W on the background of a lurid, psychedelic nude woman.

She's fun to hold.

I'm not stopping to listen for Creeper anymore. I figure he either came right after me, in contempt, or he decided to make a call for backup. If he came after me, he'd be here by now. At the very least, I figure I should hear trees falling.

No, a Bluefish-sponsored posse of sweat suit-clad gunman and young tattooed bikers probably now hunts me, not just Creeper. I'd guess no more than fifteen, twenty minutes behind me, too. I try to think of that when my leg muscles tell me to rest. If I could accomplish the task without getting wet, I wouldn't stop to pee.

Twice I catch sight of the paved road I traveled with Mama Bones, Gianni, and Thomas last night, glimpses that tell me I'm definitely on a right course. Eventually I have to hit the Parkway. Five miles. Ten miles. I don't know how far it was, or how fast I can negotiate this scrub pine and fall-red poison oak, but I'm going in the right direction.

I decide against using Gianni's prepaid cell phone. At least not just yet. I'm not much of a multitasker, and for now, moving as quickly, efficiently, and quietly through this forest deserves no less than one-hundred percent of my attention.

I'd equate the situation with parachute-jumping. Throw yourself out of an airplane, it's probably a smart idea to focus on the rip cord.

Around noon, with a windy cloudy sky announcing the arrival of darker weather, I realize I have to rest. My heart and lungs can't spread enough oxygen to counteract the exhaustion cramping my legs and back. Plus I'm already lying down.

Taking the first of an intended parade of slow, deep breaths, I notice bloody scratches now mark the backs of both my hands. Reminds me of the last time I tried to touch Susan's breasts.

My blood still screams for oxygen but I hold my breath when I hear people whispering. Two, maybe three voices. Very close. Why didn't I hear their footsteps?

Should I run for it? Or hide? Or piss my pants?

The wind picked up half an hour ago. The sky turned to charcoal over the last fifteen minutes. And now, although I guess it could be my stomach, to the south I hear a garbage-truck rumble of thunder.

Run or hide? A cloudburst makes the decision for me.

It's midnight under Gianni's black plastic. An undiluted kind of eerie darkness that makes me dizzy, uncertain of my direction or status. Kinda like waking up on Sunday with a naked stranger.

The wind pushes rain through the pines in a steady, unsettling, loud hiss. Water splashes hard against the tarp that covers me. I smell pine resin and a sticky, fearful odor I finally connect to my own perspiration. I'm sweating like it's the last day of the month and my commissions don't match my bar tab.

Two sets of soft feet creep toward me across the wet, needle-covered forest floor. My heartbeat quickens, and the thumping is so intense, I worry the noise will give me away. Like Poe's "Tell-Tale Heart."

The gentle footsteps glide past, the searchers apparently seeing only black shadow beneath fallen pine trees, one stubby trunk leaning atop the other. I'd rather be in my apartment, sure, my bed in particular, but I am kinda proud of this hiding spot. Like when I was ten and built a cool fort.

Lightning cracks the air. When my ears stop ringing, the footsteps are gone.

It's an hour or so later. The rain comes only in gusts now, peaking when the wind surges, beating like a hundred tom-toms against the dead wood and plastic over my head. The air inside my makeshift tent smells only of pine resin, not my stinky sweat.

I think my glands are empty.

My fingers grip another of Gianni's gifts, that prepaid cell phone. I'm going to take a calculated risk and make one call. The calculation being, if I don't make this call, I'm most likely going to die today or tomorrow among these sap-oozing pine trees.

I give the hospital operator Luis's room number.

"Hola."

"Luis. How's your head?"

"Austin? It is difficult to understand you. Is this perhaps a bad connection?"

"I'm whispering. I asked about the condition of your *cabeza*."

"Oh. Si. Well...still attached to my neck, I am told. In fact I am being discharged as we speak. It is fortunate for me that you have called. Perhaps you could drive to the hospital and pick me up?"

I cough. "Uh...actually, Luis, I was kinda hoping you could pick me up."

THIRTY-FOUR

At first the growl feels like part of the storm, a base ingredient of the pounding thunder. Wind and rain against the pine needles; water drumming on the ground. Even my heartbeats help mask the low-pitched rumble.

But as I work farther east, slipping stealthily from tree to bush and then back to tree again—think Elmer Fudd stumbling after Bugs Bunny—the rain gradually diminishes and a steady, background hum becomes loud and distinctively rhythmic.

It's a familiar noise, one that quickly eases the tension in my neck and shoulders.

Car and bus tires race across cement.

I've found the Garden State Parkway.

Hiding under that tarp as long as I did—I look at it as more of a strategic retreat, really—I'm hoping Bluefish's posse thinks their prey escaped. Or at least that I headed in another direction. If they play the percentages, they should have split into smaller hunting parties by now, shifted to multiple locations.

Besides "NYPD Blue," I watch the cable channels a lot. Special Forces stories are my favorite, although I find "Cooking with Emeril" fulfilling as well. What this training tells me, if I'm full-boat Carr lucky, Bluefish's Team of Terror has given up looking for me on this direct route to the Parkway.

Of course, luck hasn't exactly been my long suit lately.

Good thing I'm not in any real danger.

Emotionally, these last fifty yards are going to be the toughest.

Do I break for the fence or not? I'm torn between fear and greed. Kinda like being a day trader. I can see the Parkway traffic passing south, see the bordering fence has no barbed wire, even that the grass apron is wide and long enough for Luis to pick me up here. But if I were Bluefish, this spot due east of the lodge is exactly where I would station one of my details.

I check the time on my cell phone. Notice how everything's mine now, not Gianni's. That's because I just lugged this bag and its contents through an insurgent-held neighborhood of the Pine Barrens.

I've earned this stuff.

The digital phone tells me four-fifty-four. Good. I still have over an hour before Luis said he'd be here.

The stench of gasoline exhaust chokes my throat as I grip the chain link fence. I throw my right leg atop the five-foot barrier and use toes and arms to hoist myself over.

That wasn't so bad. I've had worse trouble mounting women.

I stumble when I land, though, capsizing onto wet grass. My thick jacket cushions the blow, but a sharp rock stabs my shoulder as I roll away from the landing. Ouch. Those military TV shows make everything look so safe and easy. Who knew you could get hurt hopping a fence?

A single star shines between drizzling clouds. And then, through the same hole in the fading storm, the moon grins at me from an eerie angle, a twisted curve reminiscent of Creeper as jack-o-lantern. The breeze, suddenly colder, chills my gut.

THIRTY-FIVE

A thin yellow beacon extends into oncoming traffic when I depress the button. I keep the flashlight on three beats, off for the same. Kind of like humping when I'm trying to extend my performance time: It definitely helps to employ techniques and devices.

I couldn't remember exactly which Parkway exit Gianni used last night—something south of sixty-three—so Luis suggested I blink the flashlight off and on between six o'clock and six-fifteen. If we don't hook up, I'm to hide, er...retreat again until seven, do the same fifteen-minute drill then.

It's six-o-five. Nothing yet. The headlights zip by me in flourishing numbers, Atlantic City drawing its usual and dedicated contingent of Saturday night gamblers. Imagine focusing all that energy—all those quarters—on some major world problem? Imagine the resources the right organization could muster?

Stop Hunger for Infinity Through Slots. Well, maybe S.H.I.T.S. isn't such a great acronym.

I blink the flashlight again. Wish the thought occurred to me earlier, say while Luis and I made our plans, but what if one or more of Bluefish's men is making regular trips down this part of the Parkway, too? Waiting for just such an obvious signal as my flashlight?

They don't know I have a cell phone, of course, that I can call for help. But why would they rule it out? And lost in the Pine Barrens, where else would I meet someone, if not just north of the exit I used last night?

I'm worrying too much. No way this baseball team from hell, the Branchtown Bluefish, is looking for me here. They walked right past me, then must have doubled back because I never saw them again.

Luis will be here any minute anyway.

A tall pair of headlights flash their high beams, an answer to my latest signal. The vehicle slows, kicks on its orange emergency blinkers, and searches for parking near my position by the fence.

Sure the hell hope this is Luis. Although actually, at this point, I'd take even Susan.

A soft night breeze brushes cool against my cheeks and neck. My knees ache from crouching.

I recognize Luis's Jeep and breathe happy for the first time all day. My lips spread into a grin.

When the Jeep's wheels stop rolling, I scramble up the grassy incline. My legs balk with weariness. My arms and hands sting with scratches. I try to forget my exhaustion and pain, keep my intent focused on safety—that red Jeep's back door.

Who is that riding shotgun? Sure ain't Umberto.

I yank at the back door handle, bend my butt to stuff myself inside. The interior light stays off. I understand the concept, but the darkness starts a shiver. My driver and front passenger show me only outlines.

"Hurry," Luis says.

Is that a woman next to him? Looks like it. In fact, I'm thinking the shape seems familiar, her hair, I mean, the way...

A meteor rips the right shoulder of my jacket and cobwebs the window beside Luis's head. Popping glass and the sharp crack of gunfire hit my ears a fraction of a second later. My heart rate doubles.

I yank shut the Jeep's back door. Wonder if that meteor could have been a bullet. Think?

Luis's front seat passenger leans out her window. She's got something in her—

Bang. Bang. Bang. Her three, return-fire gunshots light up the woman's face, the interior of the Jeep, even the edge of the forest. Oh, my. Her two-handed grip and rapid sturdy shooting tell me Walter's new replacement, Franny Dahler, has fired many a handgun at hostile forces.

Ms. Strawberry an experienced shooter?

The Jeep's engine races when Luis stomps the accelerator. Our ass-end fishtails down the slope before catching purchase in the grass. Five seconds later we're on the Parkway, free and clear.

THIRTY-SIX

I've seen her gun, so the badge isn't much of a surprise. Like love and marriage, the two are supposed to go together. What makes me squint, blink, crane, and refocus is the curious and voluminous expanse of Ms. Strawberry's law enforcement specialties, each one clearly detailed for me on her slick, anchor-weight and permanently laminated government identification card.

Frances Dahler Chapman not only holds a captain's rank with the New Jersey State Police, and is therefore automatically the Garden State's best-looking Jersey Trooper, Ms. Strawberry also carries the title of Special Prosecutor for the Governor's Select Task Force on Organized Crime, and was graduated magna cum laude from the Federal Bureau of Investigation's Advanced Weapons Training School in Quantico, Virginia.

Oh my. I'm talking to the Queen of Jersey cops.

"Why did your majesty want an undercover job at Shore Securities?" I ask.

I get a sneer, more contempt in her green eyes than her twisted lower lip, and Ms. Strawberry takes her identification back. She and I face each other in the Viking-hall kitchen of what she earlier described as a State Police safe house.

"Why the hell do you think?" she says. "Shore is the absolute center of this corrupt mess. Where else would I want to be?"

I can't get over the sudden changes. Sexy Ms. Strawberry in the bar becomes big hitter, Walter's all-business replacement, then becomes a pistol-packing state cop hunting mafia dons. The X-Men have nothing on Franny Dahler. Or Chapman. Or Ms. Strawberry. Or whatever the hell her name is.

III

"What corrupt mess?" I say.

"Illegal gambling, prostitution, fencing stolen goods, counterfeit securities, extortion, burglary, fraud, murder, and conspiracy," Franny says. "I'm just getting started. Want me to continue?"

I place my hands on the kitchen table where we sit, a swimming-pool-size octagon of thick, polished hand-pounded copper, and spread my fingers like I'm checking the polish on my nails. Nonchalant. "You think Shore's involved in all that stuff?"

"Probably. Or about to be. The spoils of an ongoing war."

The copper table shines like a gold wedding ring. Some safe house the Jersey Troopers have staked out for themselves. A rock star's retreat would be more apt. Twenty giant rooms of English Tudor inside a secluded, five-acre forest, a dock on the Navasquan River. The raw land has to be worth $10 million.

Speaking of *dinero*... "So those commission runs you showed Carmela are just bullshit?" I say. "Shore Securities is still missing one big hitter?"

"That's right. I'm a cop, not a broker."

Did my query sound that stupid? I guess maybe. It's just that I have certain business responsibilities, certain financial priorities. "And you're going to stay with us...undercover?"

Ms. Strawberry sips her third mug of premium coffee. "Probably not after tonight." She ordered some older guy named Stuart to brew a fresh pot. Stuart, probably with the Troopers thirty years, forced to search cupboards, grind and measure Colombian beans, satisfy some thirty-year-old cutie with a Trenton State law degree. "Why?" Ms. Strawberry says. "You thinking about outing me to your mafia friends?"

Maybe his boss found out Stuart voted Republican in the last election.

"Of course not," I say. "I'm thrilled you want to put Bluefish away. The bastard threatened my children."

"My job isn't to help you, Carr. Although I easily could, and might, if you cooperate with me."

"For instance?"

"For instance, was anyone in the lodge when you saw Max Zakowsky torturing this Gianni person?"

Pieces of gold sparkle inside Ms. Strawberry's sea-green eyes. She's wearing a white blouse tucked inside blue jeans, two-inch black heels and a gray tweed coat. Oh, yeah. And a tan leather shoulder holster.

"No," I say.

Hardly Carr-like patter, I know, but I feel lucky to make noise. I'm still stunned by this woman's previously undisclosed identity and intentions. Like the time my little sister's new babysitter turned judo-meister while shaking my hand, twisting my thumb 'til I yelped and flopped myself onto the carpet.

"Did you see Bluefish at the restaurant last night in Brooklyn?" she says.

"No."

"What about Mama Bones?"

"No," I say. Maybe a little too quickly.

Franny's head slowly shakes. Her light copper hair catches highlights from the chandelier. "I've already explained that lying to me is a crime. I'm giving you one more chance to tell me the truth. Not sure why. Maybe I like your gorgeous smile."

I smell sarcasm. Don't get me wrong. I have more than a little faith in the full-boat Carr grin. It's pulled me out of many tight and ugly spots. But this time I just don't think she means it.

"We already know it was Mama Bones in that Escalade," Franny Dahler says, "so do yourself a favor, don't tell me you didn't see her at that restaurant. You saw her plenty because she had to be the one dragged your skinny ass out of Brooklyn."

Skinny ass? Now I have a skinny ass?

Over the course of my so-far semi-wasted life—everything but Beth and Ryan has been pretty much a disaster—I've found the best way to lie involves actually believing your own bullshit. You must make yourself deeply and truly accept the stink icing you are about to spread over simple righteous cake.

"I see Mama Bones all the time," I say. "Mr. Vick asked to me to keep an eye on his mother while he was in Tuscany. But it wasn't Mama Bones who pulled me out of that restaurant."

Invisible fingers tug on Franny's square-ish, magazine-cover jaw, stretching the skin. A threat sparkles in her green eyes. "You're shielding a gang who wants to kill you, Carr. Who *will* kill you, and maybe your children, unless you let me protect you. But I cannot arrange your safety if you won't cooperate."

She searches my face for signs of intelligence.

It's a long and fruitless journey.

THIRTY-SEVEN

Gaunt lines condense Luis's ancient face, as if the five or so pounds he lost in the hospital pushed his Native American features back further in time. His piercing, roasted-coffee eyes shine even sharper. Hawkish.

"It is my experience that only under most unusual and extreme circumstances should one say no to the *Federales*," Luis says. "Perhaps only if they ask, 'Would you like a blindfold?'"

After encouraging me and Luis to step outside and talk privately, Ms. Strawberry—Ace Jersey Trooper—watches us from inside the warm and massive kitchen, her gaze unflinching behind the side door's glass window. Framed and pretty as a picture.

"Did you just make a joke?" I say to Luis.

"Are we not laughing?"

Luis not only looks more ancient, I think he's getting prehistorically mystical on me. I shiver. It's cold out here on this little side-entrance porch.

"They're *State-erales* by the way, and I ask again, Luis, how the hell did the New Jersey Troopers get involved? I requested you and your Jeep, not Franny Dahler. Or Chapman. Or whatever the hell her name is."

Trooper-Coffee Maker Stuart smokes a cigarette maybe forty yards away from us, snug in his North Face jacket, pacing east and west along the edge of the maple and oak forest. Silver vapors rise from his burning tobacco. Stuart's rubber soles squish on a soggy blanket of decades-old fallen leaves.

"*Cap-i-tan* Chapman overheard our telephone conversation," Luis says. "She marched into my hospital room with her many men and demanded that she be included in your rescue. What was I to do?"

"She must have been showing off for her troops. Wanting to come along for the potential shootout. But how did she overhear our conversation? Did she say my cell phone was tapped?"

"I think my hospital room," Luis says.

His breath materializes as it glides through the yellow porch light. Must be in the low forties outside on this exposed cement slab. Lucky there's no wind. My nuts would freeze up and fall off like early flower buds.

I turn my gaze on Franny inside the house. Definitely a hard edge to her, those now-frosty green eyes, but certainly a knockout. That copper-blonde hair all fluffy around her chiseled face. I don't like that she tapped Luis's phone, though.

"Your anger is misplaced," Luis says. "Without the capitan's covering fire tonight, the rifleman's bullets would have found us."

I nod. I must have been frowning at her. "You're right. I think both of you saved my life. Thanks for showing up, risking yourself."

"Thank you for seeing your error. It is clearly your most admirable quality. Now please explain to me why you will not identify this Mama Bowls."

So my pal Luis Guererro does want me to flip state's evidence. No wonder Ms. Strawberry let us have this private time together. "One big reason, Luis. Mama Bones, B-O-N-E-S, saved my life last night. Two, she's Mr. Vick's mother. A friend."

Luis's penetrating gaze seems to have texture as it passes into my soul. My eyes itch from the transmission. Must be some kind of ancient Toltec thing. Luis saying, "But it is better I think that we let the police arrest Bluefish, is it not?"

"Better than what?"

Luis's careful gaze rises to the block of pure starlight between the roof of the Tudor and the thick forest. "Better than killing him. Even success could bring us failure."

Hard to argue with that. "I can't give up Mama Bones, Luis. Not after what she did for me."

Luis eyes a star he likes. "Then we will have to kill Bluefish," he says. "Only your testimony could make the capitan arrest him now and save us this task."

I don't like it. "Why can't I just hide out for a week or two, hope

Captain Franny puts Bluefish away without my help?"

Luis brings his gaze back to earth. He nods at me, resigned, but his face stays hopeful. Has my favorite bartender thought of something I failed to consider? Or am I about to once more sense the touch of Luis's ancient Toltec magic?

"What if you only pretend to identify this Mama Bones?" he says.

Pretend? "What exactly do you mean, pretend?"

"You've made the right move, Carr," Franny says an hour later. "But are you sure you want Detective Mallory to know you're staying with me until I can assemble a State Grand Jury? I don't have to tell anybody locally."

"No, I want you to tell Mallory," I say. "He's in touch with my children."

THIRTY-EIGHT

A metallic click-click snaps open my eyes.

Paranoid imagination? Or could that have been the latching apparatus on my Trooper-assigned bedroom door? Or maybe I'm still dreaming. I swear there was just a giant robot grasshopper in the hall. Like on that episode of "Star Trek Voyager."

Why don't these aliens just knock?

Thick blackout curtains keep the midday sun at bay, the darkness thick, slowing my herky-jerky rise to consciousness. But I can't help waking up entirely when something or someone slides inside my room and gently seals the door behind them. Fear gooses my heart rate.

After the briefest shaft of hall-light, darkness again hugs me close. I breathe without making a sound. Clothes rustle nearby. Soon I hear the soft intimate whisper of a woman's breathing. I smell her lilac perfume.

Captain Franny's weight on the edge of the bed draws me to her, and her body heat toasts me through sheet and thick cotton blanket. Slowly, she slides an arm and a leg over me and tugs at the fabric between us.

"Don't say a word," she says.

While *El Capitan* nibbles my chest, rubbing her breasts across my stomach, I consider this naked Trooper's potential motivations.

Hmm. Let's see. Hmm.

Well, after admittedly incomplete deliberations, I figure either Franny fell in love with the full-boat "phony" Carr grin, or this is one of those top-secret super special police interrogation techniques they can't show you on "Law & Order."

A method too effective to make public.

Despite being in my utmost glory—I've spent twenty odd years waiting for an uninvited woman to sneak into my bedroom for a hump—I must say Franny is definitely taking her time getting down to the nitty-gritty. If I get any more excited, in fact, we could be looking at early departure. An unscheduled culmination.

I try to steer her hips into a more accessible position, but she pulls away, quickly and completely.

Hey.

I'm left with the scent of lilac, the whisper of cloth on skin as she dresses.

"Franny?"

"We'll finish this after your State Grand Jury testimony," she says. "I believe in carrots as well as sticks."

Carrots? Sticks? Is she talking about my penis?

Next time I see Franny, maybe two, two-and-a-half-hours later, I've got my fork stuck in a three-layer stack of Stuart's blueberry pancakes.

These State Troopers sure know how to make a guy feel welcome. Although it really really makes me wonder what Stuart did to draw this duty as Franny's personal chef. I think his transgression must have been significantly worse than a poor voting record.

Anyway, El Capitan, as Luis now calls her, looks undeniably scary storming into the gray stone and black-tile kitchen this afternoon. The woman's face reminds me of Dracula stalking her castle.

"What's the matter?" I ask. I'm hoping her bad mood involves her self-denied sexual encounter with yours truly. Your chance may never come again, honey.

El Capitan glances at Stuart, then looks me straight in the eye. "Mallory tipped off Bluefish to your children's location," she says.

My fork tumbles in slow motion, pancakes and syrup flying. The steel utensil clatters hard on the stone floor, an echo that travels around the big kitchen like a parading hearse.

My right hand aches from being balled into a fist. I know she's a woman, but Franny just sold out my children, I suppose in exchange for possible career advancement. My right hand wants to make her cover-girl nose bleed.

"If you had Mallory under surveillance, his phone tapped, then you knew he was crooked, knew he might give Bluefish the location of my kids," I say. "Basically, you used my family as bait."

"You picked Mallory, not us," Franny says. "You trusted him."

"You could have told me not to."

"Why? I didn't know you. I still don't. I didn't start worrying about your kids until you told us Mallory knew where they were. We worked hard to find them since then."

Can't believe anything this woman says. "Where are they?"

"Staying with a friend of your ex-wife's an hour outside of Philadelphia."

"Give me the phone number."

"We've already called. There's no answer...yet."

An odd dizziness hits me, like I jumped up too fast after sitting too long. My eyes see faded images. Kitchen shadows in a yellowish glow. "But you're still trying?"

My voice sounds unfamiliar.

"Of course," Franny says. "And I have two detectives and eight State Troopers already on their way. Fifteen minutes out."

THIRTY-NINE

Her round backside aimed at me, the top half of her covered by gray tweed, Franny Dahler Chapman—Ms. Strawberry—listens and whispers to someone on the kitchen wall phone. My body feels weightless. Floating over a deep, dark, bottomless hole.

Luis saying, "Capitan Chapman is hearing now from her detectives."

Luis rests his hand on my shoulder. Now and then he squeezes muscle beneath my dress shirt. The sturdy weight of his grip lets me breathe slower and more deeply, like a swimmer attached to a harbor buoy. But I am so damn angry. I want to scream out the window.

"My men are inside the house," Franny says.

I push away from the table and stand. Again, that dizziness whacks me. I bend forward at the waist, but extra blood to the head doesn't help. My sickness comes from the heart. What the hell would I do if something happened to Beth or Ryan? I can't even think about it.

Outside, birds squawk. Telling me something, I'm sure. The crows and jays know something I don't.

Franny glances at me. "Someone's been inside."

"Are Beth and Ryan safe?" I say.

Franny points her palm at my chest like a traffic cop, telling me to back off. Screw you, honey. I'm not waiting my turn in a line by the curb while Beth and Ryan get run over by a bus.

"Yes. But I'm staying on," she says to the phone.

"What?" I say.

"They're going downstairs," she says to me. "They hear...noises."

"What kind of noises?"

She holds up her palm again. My jaws grind. I might yet decide to flatten that statuesque nose of hers. I take steps in her direction. Never hit a woman before. Never thought it was even possible. But Ms. Strawberry here deliberately put my kids at risk.

"Yes?" she says to the phone.

I stop close enough to smell lilac, then lean in, try to hear the mumbled voice on the other end of the phone. Franny's purple-flower perfume brings back the taste and feel of her nude body. Unfortunately, it's an image that doesn't last long.

Having children is a real damper on sex.

Franny covers the mouthpiece to speak to me. "Ryan and your wife's friend are safe. They were tied up in the basement, but they aren't injured."

My heart skips. "What about Beth?"

Franny touches my arm. The concern in her eyes cuts me into digital sections. A hundred slices vertical, a hundred slices horizontal. I begin to disassemble like cable TV on a stormy, electrical night.

"The man who tied them up also took your daughter," Franny says.

My gut makes a fist. The sound my throat issues is part howl, part growl.

"Did they identify the perp?" Franny says to the telephone.

Her gaze finds me as she listens. My face bulges with blood. I'm ready to pop.

Her slender fingers slowly cover the microphone. She says, "Sounds like our friend Max."

FORTY

He is liking the drive very much. The big rented Buick surges up and down these green hills, no effort for the big V-eight engine, or the tight steering.

Max spots the hand-painted sign only as he's whizzing by, much too late to stop. Though quickly making his decision to go back, he must still drive over a mile before finding a turnaround.

Back to those three children and their offensive sign.

Is nice day in the Pennsylvania country. Cool, but with a bright blue sky and pine-washed air Jerry said comes from Canada. The crooked oak trees and the rolling hills remind Max of semi-wooded land around Budapest. With the car windows down, the clean air blowing, even the wet-earth smell is same.

Max stops the car on a dirt pull-off. He squeezes from the driver's seat, then stands a moment to cough at a dust cloud before approaching the kids and their sign. Kids' eyes get bigger and bigger as Max walks toward them.

The boy with crew-cut hair and big hands is surely the oldest. The two girls might be his sisters. All of the kids are blond with blue eyes, all staring at Max like he was Papa come to hit them with a stick. Kids all the same.

"You want a kitten, mister?" the boy says.

The boy stands up to face Max. His younger sisters stay in their beach chairs, beat-up aluminum frames with green and white plastic strips for cushions. Lawn chairs, Jerry calls them. It's pretty cold for beach chairs.

"How many cats you have?" Max says.

"Six. All of them two weeks old."

123

"Fluffy had babies," the youngest girl says.

The crew cut boy looks very worried about Max's size and strange accent, scared maybe he'll have to protect his sisters if Max turns out to be a creepy sex pervert. Max is used to this reaction, especially from children. He stretches his mouth and cheeks into a maximum smile. Maybe showing his crooked front teeth.

"Is lucky day for Max," he says. "I have exactly six nieces and nephews. They're waiting now for presents from Uncle Max. I need a cat for each."

"You want them all?" the boy says.

"Yes. You are smart boy. Is exactly what I want. Six kittens for six nieces and nephew."

The boy glances at his sisters, then down at the black-and-white spotted smelly little cats. Squirming like cockroaches.

"Six kittens might be too much for one person, mister," the boy says. "We want them to have happy homes."

Max pulls from his pocket the Timberland wallet Jerry gave him last year for Christmas and slips out a one-hundred-dollar bill. Max knows he could just grab box of cats and walk away, but he sees no reason to upset these children. Not job, like other thing.

Max sticks out hundred-dollar bill for the boy to take. "Is cold day, and children like you must have happier things for doing than to stand here. Let me make my niece and nephews happy. They like kittens, will take home to four different houses."

The crew cut boy is finally interested in something other than Max's size and shape. His gaze focuses on the money. One hundred is many dollars for a child so young.

"You're sure they'll have a good home?" the boy says.

"Nieces and nephews love little cats," Max says. "They take very good care."

Max opens the Lincoln's trunk, blocking the children's line of sight, and then dumps smelly cats into an empty burlap bag. Lucky thing he brought extras, although for first time in hour, little girl in first burlap bag completely quiet and still.

Max pokes her leg, checking to see if she's alive. A low whimper gives Max his answer.

Eighteen miles away from where he bought the smelly cats, Max sees the river and the bridge he's approaching will be a good place.

Max steers the Lincoln off the highway when he can, works the big car down dirt roads to the base of the steel and cement bridge. The big river is fast and smooth on this side, right away deep. Plus there are lots of heavy round stones to put in burlap bag.

He parks, oozes himself out into the chilly river air. Sky is orange and gold with evening. The water smells dirty, like mud and old car tires. Birds squawking somewhere. Crows maybe. Or jays.

Max opens the trunk.

FORTY-ONE

The spring grass tastes cold and wet. I know this for a fact because I've been wrestled to the ground. My stomach, nose and mouth now burrow deep into the shady green turf.

"Where do you think you're going, Carr?" Franny says.

El Capitan seems to be the only living thing not latched on, pinning me to the lawn. Bet Luis and Stuart total three-fifty, three-hundred and seventy-five pounds, easy. Even Stuart's bomb-sniffing German Shepherd, Doris, who smells like ear cheese, has a sharp-clawed paw on my neck. I guess everybody wants a piece of the credit for my arrest and detention.

I got a little lathered up, I guess. All I could think of was wrapping my hands around Bluefish's throat. I started running.

"I asked where you were going, Carr?"

"Bluefimmsh's." Think it's my face being squashed that makes the ever-mellow Carr tones ring slightly out of tune?

"Bluefish's? Good. I'm glad," Franny says. "But instead of storming over there, getting yourself killed, how about working with me? When you go see Bluefish, my guys could have you wired up to broadcast like Geraldo Rivera. You get him to say the right thing, give me the right evidence, maybe you don't have to pick out Mama Bones for the Grand Jury."

I stop struggling against Stuart, Luis, and Doris. Not that I was getting anywhere. The three of them were too much for me, although I do believe that damn dog's paralyzing ear odor was the margin of victory. "Bluefish would be certain to check me for a wire, wouldn't he?"

"Presumably," Franny says. "But he won't find the transmitter

126

my people place in you."

I stand up. Luis and Stuart let me dust off a few dozen chunks of chocolate brown mud. "In me?"

"Nano technology," Franny says. "You won't feel a thing."

My stomach's reaction seems somewhat negative over possible venous inserts and trans-dermal implantation. My gaze starts scanning for a place to barf.

"Are you sure Bluefish will get in touch with me?" I say.

"He already did," Franny says. "While you were doing your macho jailbreak thing."

"What?"

Franny hands me a telegram with a lawyer's signature. It says Mr. Joseph Pepperman may have information of import to one Austin Carr, who is believed to be in the custody of New Jersey State Police. A private golf round and meeting is proposed for tomorrow at the Branchtown Country Club.

"Bluefish wants me to play golf?" I say.

"Damnedest kidnapping I've ever seen," Franny says.

FORTY-TWO

The little girl is not so little. She asks Max to call her Elizabeth, not Beth like her daddy and mommy call her. And the little girl has some things growing under her shirt. Not a woman yet, no. And Max is no pervert. But Elizabeth not a little girl either.

"Why are you mad at cats, Max?"

Max pushes the edge of his shovel into the soft ground, slicing a tuft of new grass, the big man wishing he didn't have to dig a hole, but glad the rain made the bad job easier. "Not mad at cats. Don't like them," he says. "Is big difference."

"How is it different?" Elizabeth says. "How, exactly?"

Max smiles. "Being mad at cats is emotional. No thinking involved. I know cats all my life and do not like for many good reasons. Is opposite of emotional. For Max, it is completely logical. Cats are mean and selfish. If they need, or just decide for any reason, they will kill and eat things. Even people."

"Those little cats you drowned couldn't eat anybody."

"Little cats grow into big cats. They eat pretty birds, torture their prey after catching. And cats do not always eat what they kill. Cats are very mean."

Elizabeth gazes at Max like she knows more than him. Superior airs, Max's mother used to say. Some women look at Max this way all his life.

"My freshman psychology book would say you might have another, even bigger reason for not liking cats, Max. Something that happened when you were a kid?"

Max stops his digging. He leans on his shovel. "Is true what you say, Elizabeth. Did your father tell you I used to be in circus? Travel all over Europe with animals and crazy peoples?"

"He said you'd been in the circus."

"When I was little boy, lions got out of their cage and killed my father. Ate most of him before we find."

"Oh, my God, Max. That's awful. I'm so sorry."

"Lion tamer Frederic say it was accident that cages got open, but lion tamer Frederic marry my mother next month in Budapest. Then lion tamer pretend to be my Daddy. Only mean. He made me sleep outside with his smelly lions."

"The same ones that ate your real father?"

"Same ones."

"Oh, my God. That's the worst story I ever heard."

Max smiles. "I got even."

Elizabeth stare at him a long time before she asks. "What did you do?"

"I tell you later. First, you tell me something." Max starts digging again, but slower than before. Bluefish call him soon. Maybe this hole is not needed. "Tell me a story about your mother and father."

"My mother and father? Why?"

"Max like stories about love. You ever see them doing it?"

FORTY-THREE

My monster tee-shot splits the eighteenth fairway. Two-sixty-five, maybe two-hundred and seventy yards. Not long enough for the rankest of professional golf tours, but sufficiently distant and pretty to impress the members of any local men's club. Present company included.

"They serve drinks on that flight?" Bluefish says.

True, my child has been kidnapped. And worrying about Beth— I imagine her alone, sick with fear—well, this father can barely consider outside stimulus, let alone enjoy golf or the thematic landscaping of the Navasquan River Country Club. Yet as any good golfer will tell you, not thinking about our physical actions is exactly how we Golf Legends earn the extra attention. We turn loose our muscle-memory. Shut off the mind's calculations and let our bodies, training, and instincts take control.

I bend over to pick up my tee. "Only beer and wine on that flight. The stews don't have enough time to serve ice."

"Ha ha ha." Bluefish's laugh possesses a certain bullfrog quality. Kind of a wet croak.

Such good buddies, Bluefish and I. Playing friendly golf. Joking on the back nine. Enjoying the outdoors together. Trust me, I don't forget one second this scaly bastard had my little girl kidnapped. At least two or three times a hole, I imagine myself spinning suddenly and burying the business end of my aluminum putter deep inside one of Bluefish's eye cavities.

But so far I've suppressed my murderous impulses. I mean, the results of such conduct would hardly improve Beth's situation, or mine, and might include some kind of gruesome death for both of us. But every once in a while, just for a split second, I get the irrational notion that Bluefish wearing a putter in his face would somehow be worth any consequence.

Actually, that's insane, not irrational. I might need to improve my grip.

I wave to my cart partner, Bluefish, that I want to stroll this hole. He can have the freaking cart to himself. The less time I spend next to Bluefish, the less chance there is I'll attack and spoil my chance to get Beth back safely.

Bluefish drives our electric geezer-mobile on ahead to help my golf game partner Al look for his ball, maybe watch to make sure Al doesn't cheat. I'll walk with Jerry, who like me put his drive in the fairway. See, Bluefish and I each have best-ball partners for this big money match. A $2,000 Nassau with unlimited presses, plus $500 birdies, sandies and one-putts. The winners could go home with enough loot for a beach front condo.

Bluefish's partner is Creeper's pal from that Brooklyn spaghetti bar, the solid-shouldered gentleman with a diamond earring. Jerry. He can't drive well consistently, or hit his irons, but Mr. Diamond Earlobe can sure the hell putt. Sank a thirty-foot twister on the seventeenth to once again tie the Bluefish-Carr Cup championship.

Al, my partner, is a nervous grandfather. Big stomach, big ass, no hair. A decent golfer, and won a few holes early. But not much help lately. His soft brown eyes grow shiftier, his golf swing jerkier with every hole since we had a beer at the halfway house. He sweats a lot lately, too. Seems there's something more than money at stake for bald, round Al.

I asked Bluefish last hole why my partner's so nervous. But like every time I bring up the subject of my daughter, Bluefish says we'll talk about that stuff later, over a Cuban cigar and brandy in the clubhouse.

"You didn't know Bluefish was such a good golfer, did you?" Jerry says.

The close-cropped Bent grass under my feet succumbs to my weight like the carpet in a Ritz-Carlton lobby. "You're the one giving your team a chance to win, not Bluefish. All day long."

"You're not too shabby yourself," Jerry says. "What are you? Like one or two over?"

I shake my head. "More like six. I'll be lucky to break eighty."

"Bullll...ssshit."

On this, the final hole, with water and trees down the right, my partner Al's tee shot soared into the lakeside forest like a migrating bird. So now, when I see Al roll from the electric cart to go find his errant bird, Bluefish right behind him, I give up my stroll in the fairway to help my partner search.

Al discovers his ball tucked against the base of a tree trunk, the ball glued to the bark by a serious clump of twelve-inch crabgrass. This is what you call your basic bad lie, probably unplayable, and thus Bluefish's dream, the reason he came along to observe. With bookie-man watching, Al will not be tempted to use the old foot-wedge. He'll have to take the penalty.

Me and Bluefish staring at him, Al calls the lie unplayable, picks up his ball, takes a drop, then selects a four-wood from his bag and lines up directly toward the green. He's planning to hit his next shot straight through the trees. Maybe Al thinks he can steer it like a Cruise missile.

"Geez, Al. Can you even see the green?" I ask.

He shrugs. "I'm lying two with the penalty. If I don't get this on, I'm out of the hole."

Tiger Woods couldn't put that ball on the green.

Me shaking my head, Al whacks his third shot into the trunk of another pine. Like an angry bumble bee, the ball whizzes dead right, ricocheting into a long pond of black murky water.

Nice shot, pard.

Bluefish saying, "Looks like the match is riding on you, Carr."

Funny, I don't feel any extra weight. Not with Beth still missing.

Al drops his four-wood onto the pine needles like it's a cigarette butt. Something he's finished with forever. He waddles closer to me. His lips are white.

"Don't let him win," he says. "Please. Don't let Bluefish win."

FORTY-FOUR

I line up a putt I think might win the match.

In case my hunch is right, I should be taking my time, measuring the task from all angles, pretend I'm at the Masters. But it's impossible to concentrate on anything but my kidnapped daughter, and I thank God this is the last hole. Soon as I finish, I'll hear how I can earn Beth's release over cigars and brandy.

Not that I'd mind walking out of here with an extra $20,000. I could buy Susan that living room furniture she always wanted.

I'm crouched fifty feet behind the hole, staring at a slick thirty-foot downhiller, maybe four or five feet of right-to-left break. Jerry shanked his second shot into the water, hit his fourth into a bunker, and then picked up to join Al on the sidelines. Bluefish already tapped in for his par after a nifty sand shot. Lucky bastard.

Everything's up to me. I have to sink this birdie putt to win the match, two-putt for a tie.

Al, who hasn't left our electric cart since his ball drowned...well, Al acts like his life depends on me knocking this in. His white lips, the way Al looked back there in the woods, the problem has to be something approaching life or death. His eyes are the size of goose eggs.

My nerves fail. I know the putt's too hard as soon as I stroke it, the damn Top Flight shooting off my club head like a bottle-rocket.

Oops.

The barking puppy takes about half of the intended four-foot break and races past the hole. Six feet beyond the target, my ball reaches a plateau, picks up more speed, and then dives off a cliff.

Behind me, Al gasps.

When my Top-Flight finally completes its gruesome charge, I lie three feet off the front edge of the green. I have twenty, twenty-five feet back to the hole for par. Gee, nice putt, Carr. What a full-boat fuck-up. You've just about guaranteed yourself a three-putt. And a financial hickey the size of a new Buick.

I turn to shrug at my partner, signal Al that I'm sorry for the lapse. But Al's not in our cart anymore.

Oh, my. There he is. Running toward the forest that borders the country club. Sprinting faster than an old fat man should.

A batch of six or eight crows bursts from the tops of two budding locust trees. A gust of wind rakes my face.

Bluefish and I stand at the edge of the thick forest where Al disappeared, and where Jerry ran in after, waving a pistol and talking on a cell phone. Wonder who he was calling?

"Let's go see what's happening, shall we?" Bluefish says.

"I don't think—"

Bluefish pokes a gun in my ear.

Doesn't take us long or far to find them. Jerry has his semiautomatic pointed at Al, the two of them inside a living room-size clearing no more than fifty feet from our carts. Al's collapsed against a tree trunk, ass on the ground, legs extended. His hands cover his face, a reddish nose playing peek-a-boo between them.

He reminds me of Pinocchio, the sad puppet's nose about to grow to the size of a walking stick.

A wave of pity hits me, and my heart ticks louder when I get closer. Al's shoulders bounce with repeated sobs. Poor old geezer's whimpering like a baby.

Or is that me?

Bluefish pushes me toward the center of the clearing. The crows are back, circling overhead, squawking at each other for flight space.

When Jerry sees me, recognizes that I'm watching him, he pulls the trigger on Al. Blood and brains gush sideways from Al's head like someone forgot to cap an electric mixer. An explosion of gore. The sound seems to come later, building, then crashing like a freight train.

Al's rag-ass body melts onto the leaves and pine needles.

I vomit like a fraternity drunk.

FORTY-FIVE

Bluefish and I smoke Punch Habanas inside a steel-walled dungeon a mile or two from the country club. Golf, booze, leather recliners, and cigars. Next he'll want to call some girls.

Bluefish, my buddy in unproductive pursuits.

On the outside, this place looked like his Branchtown horse farm's flat-roofed tack room, recently whitewashed, with two windows facing the big estate's house and stables. Inside, however, there are no windows. Plus, the gray-metal floor and walls, the way the heavy door clicks like a Federal Reserve bank vault...well, they give this room the utilitarian feel of a steel rabbit trap. A private kill zone that regularly needs hose-downs.

"When the door's shut and the alarm's set, electronic devices can't send, receive, or record signals in here," Bluefish says. "Like the commercial says, what happens here, stays here."

Wonder if Ms. Strawberry's people are really shut out? If so, true privacy facilitates new possibilities for me. "Jerry checked me before we played golf," I say. "Including my fillings. I'm not wearing any wires."

"Of course you're not," he says. "But I figure in the course of a private and friendly discussion, when I could admit to say, extortion, kidnapping, or even intended murder, why take chances?"

I nod. "Good point."

"I figure the F.B.I. or that state-cop Chapman could have some kind of miniaturized shit Jerry couldn't find, something my so-called experts never heard about."

"I suppose."

"Not that I'm callin' you a liar."

"Of course not."

"Anyways. In here, I feel free to discuss whatever."

"But if they did put some kinda miniaturized wire-thing like that on me, wouldn't they already have heard you and Jerry kill Al?"

Bluefish removes the cigar from his mouth. "You mean that gunshot? You barfing?"

I blink. Is that all Franny's implant picked up? Maybe also Bluefish saying, Let's go see? Shit.

"My pal Jerry killed a rabbit," Bluefish says. "And if they dig up what's buried in that clearing near the eighteenth hole, a shot-dead rabbit's exactly what they'll find. Our former friend Al ran off the eighteenth green instead of paying off his bet. Cheap bastard. We may never see him again."

I try not to look disappointed, but this means Captain Strawberry still has nothing she can use against Bluefish. Nothing but me. "Why'd you kill him? Not just to frighten me, I hope."

Bluefish sucks the mid-size Punch. "Like your former coworker Ragsdale, Fat Al is a degenerate gambler. Ran up his debts but couldn't pay off. He had it coming. Plus, I wanted to remind you that violence is part of my world, not yours."

He leans back and blows a fine stream of Cuban cigar smoke straight up. Like a volcano. "So what's it gonna be, Carr? You playing for my team now?"

"Excuse me?"

"You know what I'm asking. Nothing's changed."

"Oh, plenty's changed. You kidnapped my daughter."

He twists the cigar in his mouth, savoring the smooth wet tobacco. He makes it dirty, like a sex show in Tijuana. "Exactly. Now you have to do business with me."

God damned bastard. I swear I could beat him to death with a nine-iron. "Beth is all right?"

"She's fine. Now tell me what you're going to say to the state grand jury about Mama Bones? What did you already tell Chapman about me?"

I stare into Joseph "Bluefish" Pepperman's ebony gaze, a look that recalls the glass eyes in that trophy fish over the bookie's bed. Shiny black marbles. Sightless and dead. Not the kind of man you really want to do business with.

But I think I must. For Beth. And Ms. Strawberry not listening makes my betrayal a whole lot easier.

"Let Beth go, I'll say whatever you want in front of the grand jury. I give you my word."

I'm driven back to the golf course and my Camry by Bluefish's attorney, Jano Johanson, a cosmopolitan Viking with long red hair and a full red beard. He just asked me where I'm going to be later "in case your daughter is located quickly."

I should lay this redhead out, get his three-thousand-dollar suit dirty with parking lot dust. Officer of the court, my ass. Bluefish's Norseman raider is more like it. But getting Beth back safely can be my only priority, and rocking the Norseman's longboat is not a particularly aces idea now that I've made a deal with his boss.

"I'm headed back to protective custody," I say.

"You're a suspect or a material witness?" Jano says.

"I don't know."

He laughs. "Pal, I suggest you get yourself some legal representation."

FORTY-SIX

The electronic phone chime doesn't slow me down. Neither does Franny plucking a slick, black Motorola cell phone from the inside pocket of her business jacket. What works is Franny saying, "Carr. Shut up."

It's the story of my life, really. Always talking too much. Even when I've asked for the order and I know the sales manual says to keep quiet and wait; even when I should just embrace a woman and kiss her. No, whenever patience is most at a premium, whenever silence is truly golden, you can count on Austin Carr—Mr. Blabbermouth—to deliver entirely pointless and mood-busting oratory.

I get nervous, I suppose. I tend to run on, delay the moment of rejection or acceptance. It's a major flaw in the old Gift of Gab.

Franny pushes the cell phone against her ear. "Chapman."

Illegible blue symbols flash across the telephone's glossy-black screen like a stock-market tape. The late afternoon sun glows like a florescent orange ball in the louvered kitchen windows. Stuart's browning a whole chicken on an eight-burner, cast iron stove. In his white dress shirt and tie, the pot-holder mittens, Stuart could be taping a half-hour show on the Food Network.

Another Arresting Recipe from Cooking with Cops.

That's right, I'm back at Trooper Bat Cave, being bullied by Franny and cooked for by Stuart. By her own order, I was describing to Franny, for the third time, exactly how Bluefish and Jerry killed my golf-partner, Al. Although I suppose I was still specifically elaborating in some detail about my wild first putt when Franny's cell phone rang.

"Repeat that," Franny says to her Motorola.

El Cap-i-tan wears her strawberry blonde hair differently tonight, kinda pushed over to one side like a 1940s movie star. Remarkably symbolic of her general mood, actually. Obviously bent out of shape. Like the Queen of New Jersey Cops already suspects I reached some tit-for-tat with Bluefish.

Listening to her cell, whatever it was the poor man or woman had to repeat, Franny's forehead wrinkles. Now she glances at her diamond-studded Rolex. "You're certain about the subject's condition?" Her gaze lifts, finds mine. Her eyes are unreadable. Cop eyes. "I'll make sure he gets there."

I swear my heart stops. "What?"

Franny slips the phone back in her jacket on her way over. "Your daughter walked into the Rumson New Jersey police station fifteen minutes ago. Beth says she's fine, safe and sound."

My heart restarts right into double-time. "She's all right?"

"A bruise or two. Scratches on her back she says came from being locked in a car trunk. She's on her way home right now in a State Police cruiser. If you want, Stuart and I will drive you to meet her."

I throw off the anger about her being mistaken for a spare tire. She's alive. Not even seriously hurt. Thank God. Thank God. Relief chases a rock of tension from my neck and shoulders. Beth's sunny-morning blonde hair fills my mind's eye, then her untrained but genetically true, someday-famous Carr smile.

Thank God. Oh, thank God.

"You made a deal with Bluefish, didn't you?" Franny says. Her voice is a growl. Her green eyes are Fury. By the stove, Stuart slides a step farther away from us.

"I didn't make any deal." For my purposes—that is, to produce a better lie—I choose to think of my arrangement with Bluefish as an offer I couldn't refuse. Offer and deal are not the same thing. I did not make a deal.

Franny shows me a Mona Lisa smile, then grabs my forearm. She leans in close, so close her breath warms my neck. "If you don't testify against Mama Bones tomorrow, Carr, you are fucking dead."

I don't know why she's whispering. Stuart's far enough away to have different GPS numbers.

When she sees me step onto the porch, the one I built with my own hands, my ex-wife Susan becomes a gargoyle. Her nose flares. Her lips, eyes, and ears pull back into a mask of ferocity. Fangs flashing.

Reminds me of our infrequent sexual encounters.

Susan saying, "You are dead to these two children, Austin. Do you hear me?"

I think the ex-wife might be upset.

"What happened to Beth is your fault, you miserable, slime-sucking worm," she says.

Definitely upset. But Susan never cursed like this before. Her only four-letter word was dead. Must be that new boyfriend Ryan told me about at dinner a few weeks ago. Can't remember the turkey's name. The Presbyterian minister that goes to AA meetings.

Susan lets Ms. Strawberry inside the house, but blocks my path. Well, this could be a problem. Not only does Susan weigh enough to give me a good wrestle, but if I'm forced to push past her, lay hands on her, I'd be in violation of my court order. Possibly committing a crime.

A surreptitious elbow may be needed to precipitate my crossing of the threshold. There. And a wee-bity little shove. I came to see my daughter Beth and that's exactly what—

Franny knees me in the nuts. Then she throws a forearm under my chin, grabs my belt, and throws her weight into my Adam's apple and my belly at the same time. Whoa. She governs my center of gravity like Tom Glavine controls a baseball. Lifting and pushing...oh, my...back we go.

Franny's bum rush forces us both outside, narrowly missing Susan, but El Cap-i-tan doesn't stop until I'm sailing off the porch, a stooge in this unfilmed version of the World's Greatest Bartender. Even my kids know who Mr. T is, but I remember when he won the rowdy-customer toss championship hands down.

And what a shove by Ms. Strawberry. I'm on the cement walkway leading to Susan's porch, looking up at Franny Dahler. Franny Chapman. El Cap-i-tan.

"When you feel like getting up, go wait in the car, Carr," she says.

Fun-ny.

FORTY-SEVEN

Understanding and maturity often arrive late in a boy's life. Like youth, dreams are hard to leave behind.

But when dawn comes, and he finally grasps his life will never involve Big Money, that $500,000 European sports cars, million-dollar yacht parties, and famous beauties like Shania Twain are forever beyond his reach...well, that's when a boy becomes a man.

At least I sure the hell hope so. Because it's about time I grew up. Way overdue, in fact. See, worrying about my testimony tomorrow before a special state grand jury, it occurs to me, were I rich like I always figured I should be, I'd have a hotshot attorney postponing my appearance, or otherwise devising some totally legitimate loophole to excavate my ass.

But no, Big Money is not mine. I can't afford an unbeatable mouthpiece. I never will. Nice things like top-shelf defense attorneys are forever beyond my reach. So is Shania Twain. I believe I understand this now. The Fast Lane down Easy Street is closed to Austin Carr.

Tomorrow, I can either identify Mama Bones and make Franny happy, or I can somehow not identify Mr. Vick's gray-haired mother and make Bluefish Mr. Smiley Face.

The consequences of both are obviously the subject of some concern. If I please Franny, Bluefish might kill not only me, but probably Beth, Ryan, Susan, Susan's friends and neighbors, not to mention everybody's lawns, dogs, and goldfish. On the other hand, if I fulfill my verbal agreement with Bluefish and refuse to point the finger at Mama Bones, Franny has promised me jail time for perjury and conspiracy to commit murder.

Why can't one of my options be careful and supervised use of a reliable time machine? Why can't I go back to that afternoon in Luis's restaurant and tell Bluefish "fine" when he first mentions doing business with Shore?

At least it's nice to know I've reached maturity.

I take my mattress off the bed in my Trooper mansion bedroom and lean that sucker against the wall. I start with a few kicks, then step closer and start punching, right, left, right, left, until my arms are tired and I go back to kicking, kicking, kicking until my legs feel like wet cement.

I take up punching again.

I go on like this for, I don't know, half an hour. When all four of my limbs are numb with exhaustion, I crumble to the floor. My mouth is open. I'm panting. Sweating.

Tears slowly fill my eyes. When the water finally overflows and tickles my cheeks, I stand up, fists trembling, and bellow like a wounded bear for all my lost dreams.

"Shania!"

FORTY-EIGHT

"Could you repeat the question, please?"

Quiet, individual sighs blend into a raucous, collective groan that echoes around the oak-paneled Trenton courtroom like a barking pit bull. The wave of verbal animosity finally crashes over me and dissipates.

Seems my dumb responses and other delaying tactics wear thin on the assembled State Grand Jury. Gee, I've only been on the witness stand two hours. And I've already given them my name and address.

"Mr. Carr, please pay attention," Franny says. "This is very important. You're taking up the grand jury's time. Now, once again, look around the courtroom. Do you see the woman who had Anthony Farascio's body removed from Butch's restaurant that night?"

Franny sports quite the courtroom demeanor. Impressively dressed. Authoritative. Articulate. In possession of all the facts. And pissed as hell at me for dragging this out, although staying very much in control for her audience.

"Please, Mr. Carr. Look at the target of this investigation. Do you see that woman from the restaurant here today?"

I have to admire the way Franny uses word emphasis. Every gaze in the courtroom focuses on Mama Bones. Hard not to, the way Franny drags her description out. I've heard any good prosecutor includes acting classes in his or her training, but Franny might need an agent.

I stare at Mama Bones. Her gray hair. The sharp eyes that miss nothing. And dressed today like the sweetest grandma you ever saw, including blue hair, hand-knitted shawl, and aluminum walker.

"Mr. Carr. Please."

Guess it's time to get this over with. I take one last deep breath before I drop the five-hundred pounder: "I can't be sure."

Franny's cheeks flush. "What did you say?"

I search the back of the courtroom for something to focus on. I memorize the details of the double-door's right side, the six-inch brass hinges. "I said I can't be sure it's the same woman."

El Cap-i-tan's sea-green eyes burst into flames. The small courtroom barks again with whispered conversations. A knot expands inside my gut. Reminds me of the time I farted at Susan's parent's Christmas dinner.

Franny almost spits at me. "Mr. Carr, you identified this woman, by name, on two...no, three separate occasions. In your sworn statement to my office, in fact, you described Angelina Bonacelli exactly, and swore under oath, on the Bible, that you'd known this woman by sight for more than seven years."

I nod in complete agreement. "Of course I know Mama Bones. She's the mother of my business partner, Vick Bonacelli. I just don't know for sure she was the woman in that restaurant."

Franny snatches some papers off the prosecutor's table. "You were certain before. My transcript shows you voluntarily mentioned Angelina "Mama Bones" Bonacelli—by name—as the woman who supervised the disposal of Anthony Farascio's body."

What drama. Franny's long pointing finger reminds me of Madame Lafarge.

"Yes, that's true," I say. "That's what I thought. What I'm saying now is, though, I can't be sure the woman in that restaurant was the same woman I see sitting here today. I just can't be certain."

Franny's cheeks puff like balloons. Then air hisses out between her teeth like a punctured tire.

FORTY-NINE

Franny Chapman trashes her empty Starbucks cup, snaps open her briefcase, and seizes a red manila folder. My aces lawyer, Randall Zimmer, Esq., begins to tap the eraser-end of his pencil on a new pad of lined yellow legal paper. The preliminaries are over. It's time, lady and gentleman, for the main event.

Franny pushes an eight-by-ten glossy photograph at us across the polished walnut desk. After handcuffing me in the grand jury room and locking me up, not letting me use the telephone for three hours, Franny now has questions. A minor Chapman-Zimmer skirmish in the hallway was followed by calmer negotiation which led to the three of us sitting down in this courthouse conference room.

"Talbot told you about the A.A.S.D. report she'd prepared," Franny says. "You knew those co-mingling charges would ruin your business. But when you went to her room that night, you probably weren't intending to kill her. So what happened? You argued and lost your temper?"

I glance at the photograph. It's a black-and-white shot of Anne Marie Talbot after the murderer choked and burned her, a close-up of her barbecued head. At least that's what the black-marker printing says on the back. Could be a horror-movie prop, or a ruined, bone-in roast. The disgusting, barely human thing seems to be oozing some kind of black gravy.

Mr. Zimmer saying, "My client's alibi is well established, Ms. Chapman. Should you decide to prosecute him for Ms. Talbot's murder, you will in fact be the first witness I depose."

Zimmer's hawk-like eyes are the same dark caramel as the walnut desk. Looking at him, feeling the love, I am deeply and truly sorry for every lawyer joke I ever told. When you need one, a clever, juiced, and tough-in-the-clinches attorney can save your sorry ass. Spending the big bucks goes down easy when your job or even a prison sentence's at stake. Right this second, having Mr. Z for a champion glows inside me like a double-shot of forty-year-old bourbon.

"Would you mind looking this over as well?" Franny says. She shoves a three- or four-page document at me, loose pages stapled together in the upper left corner.

Despite Mr. Z's mighty parry and thrust, El Cap-i-tan's green eyes shine with confidence. I saw a lightning flash of defeat in the Grand Jury room earlier, but now Ms. Strawberry's back on offense, certain of her superior firepower and numbers. God, I love strong women.

I pick up the stapled papers wondering what the hell Franny throws at me now, but I wait until Mr. Z gives me the okay before I read. If you're paying five-hundred an hour for advice, it's important to listen. Lawyers also like you better, work harder, when you follow orders. Especially big German ones.

Page one is like a cover sheet. A centered title. Oh, my. I've never read a Forensic Pathology Summary before. Must be like an autopsy report.

Should I put on rubber gloves?

FIFTY

OFFICE OF THE MEDICAL EXAMINER
Seaside County, N.J.

Forensic Pathology Summary

> *Body No. 244: Talbot, Anne Marie*
External Examination
> *Body is clothed in a green, acetate-rayon dress which has been scorched, melted and destroyed along the tops of both shoulders. Burns are visibly consistent with position of body to portable charcoal burner and fire damage at scene.*
> *A hand-lens examination of the burned fabric reveals loose fragments of victim's carbonized tissue. Body is wearing no undergarments, stockings, or shoes.*

I glance up at Franny. "Talbot didn't strike me as the kind of woman who dressed commando."

"Maybe you raped her and kept her panties as a souvenir," Franny says.

So much for playing Sherlock. Back to my perusal.

I think Franny's mad she didn't get to award me her previously offered carrot.

Body is that of an adult female Caucasoid, sixty-five and one-half inches in length, one-hundred twenty-nine pounds in weight. Outward appearance consistent with stated age of thirty-four years. Hair and eye-color are indeterminable due to carbonization and / or destruction of all indicative facial and cranial tissues. Portions of the left sphenoid bone, left eye orbit, the left zygomatic bone and arch, as well as the left portions of the maxilla and mandible are exposed and burned.

Visible contusions on victim's neck suggest manual strangulation prior to burning, although condition of surviving tissue prevents observation of typical asphyxia results, i.e., broken facial capillaries and / or cranial hemorrhaging.

Examination of oral cavity reveals absence of all teeth and indications of prior elective removal. Matches dental records of stated victim.

Visible carbonization and destruction of tissue on thumbs and fingers. Suggests effort to prevent or delay identification.

Back and buttocks unremarkable.

There are no tattoos or significant scars.

Rigor mortis is firmly established. Lividity is prominent and consistent with position of body at scene.

The internal examination tells me more than any normal person would want to know about liver weight and stomach contents, but a couple of phrases catch my eye. One, the doc's exam of the respiratory system "strongly indicates manual strangulation as cause of death," and two, all of Anne Marie's burns were "administered post-mortem."

Choke dead, then burn. Kinda like kicking a dead horse. Suggests a lot of anger to me.

"What I find interesting is that the woman may not be Anne Marie Talbot at all," Zimmer says. "You don't even know the victim's eye color."

Guess Mr. Z was reading over my shoulder.

"The DNA results are due tomorrow," Franny says.

Mr. Z shoots up from his chair, nods for me to stand beside him. "Then call us when your intuition becomes reality. Mr. Carr is done with your questioning for today. And he will no longer accept protective custody."

"The body is Anne Marie Talbot," Franny says. Without getting up, she points her right forefinger at me. "And if he didn't kill her, he knows who did."

Mr. Z glares at her. "The truth is, Ms. Chapman, you are angry with my client over his testimony before the Grand Jury this morning. That anger caused you to falsely imprison Mr. Carr for several hours today. At present, I am only considering charges, but I can assure you there will be serious legal consequences if this department continues using emotion to guide its actions."

Franny doesn't blink. "Are you curious what I think is interesting about this forensic summary?"

Zimmer clutches my arm. We show Franny our backs as he reaches for the doorknob. Mr. Z's manicured fingernails are as perfect as clear plastic.

"Only two reasons I know to have your teeth surgically removed," Franny says. "Singers sometimes do it for the sound, to change their tone or timbre. Prostitutes do it to give better blow-jobs."

I try to stop—gee, that's interesting about the teeth—but Zimmer pushes me through the open doorway. My right heel skids a few inches in protest.

"I think you found something in Talbot's past and tried to blackmail her into changing that report," Franny says. She finally pushes herself up from the walnut table. "When Talbot wouldn't cooperate, wouldn't let Shore off the hook, you killed her."

Over his shoulder, Mr. Z says, "You should be in Hollywood writing screenplays."

Franny peeks into the hallway as we're walking away, but Zimmer's hand is still on my elbow. Two uniformed cops strut side-by-side toward us down the otherwise empty passage. A window behind them casts moving, undefined shadows between us. Their shoes click ominously on the marble floor.

"You're going to jail very soon, Carr," Franny says. She brushes a thick strand of blonde hair behind her ear. "Murder. Conspiracy. At the very least, perjury and lying to a state prosecutor."

"Good day, Ms. Chapman," Mr. Z says.

"And maybe that A.A.S.D. report on Shore should be part of my court filings on Bluefish this afternoon."

I don't understand her threat until Mr. Z explains on the courthouse steps. If Franny includes Talbot's preliminary A.A.S.D. report in the complaint against Bluefish, Talbot's co-mingling charges against Shore will be public record. Accessible to the newspapers.

If the reporters dig it up—and it sounds like Franny will make sure they do—the headlines alone are going to bury us.

My shares in Shore Securities won't be worth the price of a first class stamp. Only scholarships will put my kids through college.

I'll be back living in a freakin' camper.

FIFTY-ONE

Clooneys bar is lousy with pretty, sophisticated women. But all the other birds fade into a gray background with Gina perched among them.

Arrow-straight, raven-shiny hair covers her ears and splits in two over each shoulder. Wonder how she lost the curls? Below a trim row of bangs, Gina's super-sized, almond-shaped eyes are shadowed like an Egyptian princess. A thick necklace of oblong gold rectangles completes the Cleopatra package.

I bow before sliding onto the stool beside her. "You summoned me, your Highness?"

Actually, Clooneys was sort of my idea. I found Gina's message saying she wanted to talk when I came home from the courthouse. I suggested a drink overlooking the ocean, maybe dinner if we found the right mood. Sure I'm kinda half in love with Franny. She'll always be Ms. Strawberry, a vision across the Martha's crowded upstairs barroom. But one-half for Franny still leaves one-half for Gina, right?

"I hear you refused to identify Mama Bones to the state Grand Jury today," Gina as Cleopatra says. Her long fingers twirl a classic martini glass.

"And I thought grand jury proceedings were secret." I check my surroundings, make sure our conversation doesn't become public information as well.

"A friend of a friend was in the room," Gina says. "She said Chapman went ballistic."

"Promised to put me away for twenty years. She's really pissed."

Gina sips her drink. "I think I might know why."

152

The bartender's gaze asks me what I want. I order a double Wild Turkey on the rocks, wondering where Gina's going with this one. Not much of a secret why Franny's feeling foul.

"Okay, I'll bite," I say. "Besides the fact I stiffed her on my testimony, maybe ruined her case, why is Captain Franny Chapman all over my ass?"

"Because she and Anne Marie were good friends. I saw them together once."

"When? Where?" My heart rate ticks higher.

"It was five or six years ago," Gina says. "I saw them at a private party in northern New Jersey. Tony went out one night to play poker. I was jealous, so when it got late I drove to his friend's, found Tony and his pals frolicking with four half-naked prostitutes. Two of them were Anne Marie and Frances Chapman—or Dahler, was she was known then."

"Why didn't you say something before?"

"I didn't put it together until this afternoon when I saw the picture of Chapman in the newspaper. It reminded me of Anne Marie, the two of them that night. That's when I left the message on your telephone."

"You're sure about this?" I say. "Talbot and Chapman were prostitutes?"

"I can't swear they were pros. But I'm positive they were two of the four girls acting like it that night. They loved it when I plastered Tony with his friend's five-thousand-dollar Tiffany lamp. Tony needed eighteen stitches."

How did two mob party girls find their way into such unlikely government and semi-government employ? One an investigator with the American Association of Securities Dealers, the other a captain with the New Jersey State Troopers? Could explain how Franny knew about Talbot's tooth-removal trick.

Or is Gina delivering a ton of horseshit here?

If so, why?

"Let's pretend you're right," I say. "How does Anne Marie's past play into her murder? Is it connected to Franny being so hot to put Bluefish away?"

Gina raises an eyebrow. "Oh, it's *Franny* now?"

Oops. I give her the full-boat Carr sheepish grin. "I was locked up with her for two days. I got tired of calling her captain."

"Sounds like you two got to know each other pretty well." Gina smiles like she knows what happened in my bedroom Sunday afternoon.

My bourbon arrives. I taste it. Still the same. Like the Kentucky woods, dark and sunny at the same time. "Well, it was close. But I didn't play my cards right."

Gina laughs, and then leans across the space between us and kisses my cheek. Her lips are cool against my skin. "You're cute," she says.

Sexy would be my first choice. Cute doesn't make the top ten. But all in all, cute ain't bad. I've certainly been labeled by worse adjectives. Silly. Stupid. Sexually retarded, I found most objectionable.

Gina finishes her martini. "I heard something else, too. The story Mama Bones told you was right. The initial Branchtown Police investigation did find a DVD and recording equipment in the next hotel room. The equipment was connected to a tiny hidden camera in Talbot's room. Supposedly, the DVD showed the actual murder."

"How could that be?" I say. "I mean, wouldn't they have arrested the murderer by now?"

"The cops claim to have lost it," Gina says. "That's why Detective Mallory was suspended and will likely be indicted. The Seaside County prosecutor thinks Mallory destroyed the DVD to protect someone."

"Where did you hear this?"

"Same person that was inside the Grand Jury room today. That friend of a friend."

"Pretty impressive information, Gina. Think your friend knows what she's talking about?"

"I'd say you can count on it. Shall we order dinner? I'm starving."

I make my move after dessert, suggesting a nightcap at my apartment. Unfortunately, Gina's not buying, and frankly I'm a little surprised. Not only did I maintain the full-boat Carr grin for over an hour, but she called me, right? I can't believe she agreed to meet just so she could tell me about Anne Marie and Franny being party girls.

"I like you, Austin, and God knows my marriage was in bad

154

shape when Tony died. But it's just too soon for me to be dating. Try me in six months."

Right. In six months Gina will be married again and pregnant with twins.

I should have cut the grinning and just kissed her.

FIFTY-TWO

Carmela hands me a twice-folded section of newspaper. I try not to think of her as Ms. Butterface anymore because I understand it's sexually demeaning. But Vick's daughter has on a scooped-neck, tight yellow sweater, and her scoops are bulging from their sugar cones. My horny-boy eyes require a hard sell to wrap themselves around a newspaper.

I stand behind Shore's trading desk, unable to sit or focus on gray printed matter.

"This is page ten of today's *New York Times*," Carmela says. "A friend woke me up at five o'clock this morning to read it to me."

Here's the thing about guys and breasts: If the FCC would allow it, a television channel with nothing but naked boobs would win every ratings sweep. No male above the age of seven would watch much else.

"Stop staring at my tits and read," she says.

Oops. "Sorry, Carm."

"I knew I shouldn't have worn this sweater."

I didn't have my coffee yet this morning, and now I'm thinking why bother. The headline makes me want bourbon and tequila because I know Carmela wouldn't show me this story unless Shore is mentioned.

Grand Jury Claims Auto Shop Owner is NJ Shore Crime Boss

The story's opening paragraph—that Joseph "Bluefish" Pepperman was indicted and arrested last night following a two-year investigation by FBI and New Jersey State organized crime units—is

investor, co-mingling sounds like stealing no matter how hard you explain clearing-bank procedures and their overnight help's frequent mistakes.

Half my clients will want their accounts transferred. The other half will seek my torture and death.

FIFTY-THREE

I was wrong about the *Branchtown Sun*. Checking Mike's Newsstand on my way back to work, I learn our local paper did not run Mr. Vick's photograph on page one under the caption, "Crook." In fact, Mr. Vick's page-one headshot is captioned "Mob Ties."

Since everybody in this part of New Jersey knows Bluefish murdered his wife, and once robbed churches, the Sun's story skips the background stuff to play up his alleged connection to Shore Securities, the unsolved murder of Anne Marie Talbot, and the dead A.A.S.D. agent's allegations of co-mingling at "Bluefish's operation," the previously mentioned Shore.

Jesus. The facts are bad enough. Why do they have to make up crap? What are we, George Bush Securities?

I hear telephones ringing as I walk into Shore from the sidewalk. Yolanda, our current greeter-slash-phone monkey, is talking, writing, and listening as fast as she can, taking messages and punching flashing lights. The pink phone slips are piling up in front of her like lawn flamingos after a hurricane.

All of Shore's clients must be pulling their accounts.

I wave at Yolanda to start sending my calls through, then jog to Mr. Vick's office.

"Are you sure?" I say. "I can't believe it."

Carmela's grinning, her shoulders a brace against my office doorway. Her sweater's been exchanged for a loose-fitting blouse. "Why can't you believe it?" she says. "We've lost a total of five accounts. And none of the brokers was sorry about losing the customers."

"I can't believe it," I say. "The newspapers made us sound like La Cosa Nostra's private investment bank."

"What do you want me to say? Nobody reads the paper? I'll tell you this, Austin. The people that did read it said they knew Mr. Vick, and the paper had to be full of crap. Or, like my friend says, maybe people like being connected."

"I can't believe it."

"You said that. Three times now. Are you hungry? Want me to call out for some dinner?"

I shake my head. The stock market tape travels across my office's TV screen. The Dow was up big today. The Fed signaled they're done raising interest rates, and the institutions were buying heavy. Even individual investors jumped in. That's why the phones were busy.

"How about Chinese?" Carmela says.

"Not one of the calls I took this afternoon even mentioned the story."

"Mexican? I could send somebody to Luis's?"

Her smile reminds me of sunshine and hay. Or maybe it's the freckles and hair on her upper lip.

"Red chili burritos?" she says. "Or did Chinese sound good?"

Sounds like Carmela's been dreaming about pork lo mein, although my mind's suddenly spinning off in another direction entirely. Whoa. One of those crazy ideas that come out of nowhere. Or was it that homily Luis threw out there this morning? That concept he tossed at me, an over-polished gem about turning crisis into opportunity.

"Hold off on lunch," I say to Carmela. "If he's still alive, I want you to find Rags, get his fax number, send him a copy of both the *New York Times* story and the *Branchtown* one, the picture of Mr. Vick."

"I'm not talking to that scumbag," Carmela says. "He tried to kill me, remember?"

"You mean when he pretended to wrap that calculator cord around your neck?"

"Pretended?"

"You know he still loves you, Carm. He probably just did it to scare you...so he could crack that line about recalculating your yield to maturity."

"You're an asshole, you know that?"

"Okay, you're right. It was definitely an act of violence. Plus, I forgot you almost married the jerk. Can you just find him for me then? Get me a phone number?"

Yes, sir. A gem of an idea, Luis. Thank you. Crisis does indeed offer opportunity.

Ms. Butterface will talk to Rags. I know she knows where to find him.

I'll call Walter myself.

FIFTY-FOUR

The low black sky is a comfort to Max, the rain and thunder his oldest friends. It is the stark and glaring white sun that unnerves him. Days like today when the cloudless blue sea above has no depth and no spirit, the wind no taste. As if all life had abandoned the planet.

"Get in here and drive this God damn car," Bluefish says. "There's nothing wrong with you."

Boss was never a compassionate man. Much too self-centered, unthinking about others. But two nights in jail make him cranky like circus animal. Cage crazy. "Very sick, boss. Very bad stomach. What Jerry call squirtin' dir—"

"Enough," Bluefish says. "We'll stop and buy you some diapers. Now get in the God damned car or you're fired. We gotta pick up Jerry. I can't fucking believe you're afraid of that spic bartender."

Max sighs. Big-time asshole, what Bluefish is. Sitting in his gas-sucking Chevy Suburban. Shouting orders at Max who could break him into parts. Boss should know Max isn't afraid. Boss should respect Max's better knowledge of natural forces.

Today, the sky so pure and empty; today is a day for staying home, not for confronting enemies.

"Okay," Max says. "But give me one minute."

"No. Wait!"

Max shuts door in his room.

Inside a cigar box under his bed, his fingers clutch a sharp, hand-hewn arrowhead of flint attached to a thin leather necklace. The familiar rough skin of the stone makes him close his eyes and

163

remember the night his father presented him with a very special gift.

Slowly, using unusual ceremony, his father lifted the rock necklace over his head and placed it around Max's neck. "Thousands of years ago," said his father, "this arrowhead belonged to a wise and experienced hunter. A man with special knowledge. Carry it when you face danger, Max. The rock has a spirit inside that will protect you."

Three days after his father gave him the arrowhead, Max's father was dead. Killed by lions. Did the world's strongest man die because he gave Max the ancient rock? Something Max always wonder.

"Max, God damn it!"

Bluefish calls him from hallway.

Max stuffs the arrowhead in pocket of his jeans. Logic tells him no rock, even such an old and perfectly carved one, can protect Max from bullets.

But why would his father lie? And besides, like Jerry says, it can't hurt.

"I'm coming," Max says.

FIFTY-FIVE

Spooky how you can savagely dislike someone on initial eye contact. Their size and shape. Their expression. Don't know if the feeling's been natured or nurtured, but when instant aversion kicks me in the ass, hostility and venom rise from deep within.

My gaze locks onto a tall blond man watching the front door as I push inside Luis's Mexican Grill. Surfer Dude's wearing knee-length white bathing shorts and a blue T-shirt that says "Can I Put My Burrito in Your Taco?" yet he has the balls to sneer at me while I dance through five or six people waiting for tables.

This single, nonverbal exchange produces a lizard-brain reaction in me of distrust, fear, animosity, and adrenaline. I haven't wanted to punch a stranger this badly since April Higgins kicked my nuts first day of kindergarten. My feelings about this big blond surfer asshole aren't logical. They must be prehistoric.

"Hi, Austin."

Whoa. I'm so busy puffing macho across the noisy restaurant, I've failed to notice my bar-area co-occupant, Gina Farascio, her long black hair returned to those wavy curls that Big Daddy imagines spread out before him on a pillow. Curls-to-straight, then back to wavy curls. The lovely Gina must spend as much time doing her do as I do thinking about sex.

Well, almost.

Gina squeezes my shoulder as she leans in to buzz my cheek. Her perfume conjures a summer flower garden, and I can't help it, my hand instinctively reaches for her waist. Her flesh beneath the black cocktail dress electrifies my fingertips.

"I didn't see you when I came in," I say.

165

Gina pulls away, her gaze locked on mine. "No? What were you looking at?"

I toss her the famous full-boat Carr grin while I dream up a response. I'm looking for clever, flattering, and pithy. Let's see. How about, "I can't remember anything before you said hello."

Her midnight eyes light up like the sky before dawn.

The Gift of Gab has its moments.

I'm on a stool, my back to the front door, when the hubbub level of Luis's restaurant plunges.

I wrest my attention from Gina to glance down the bar. Dozens of faces are expressing concern. Their gazes seem to have focused on the entrance, or already lowered themselves in submission. Can't be zombies or masked gunmen. No one's screaming. Maybe it's just the threat of violence all these people are worried about.

"Bluefish," Gina says.

I swivel more, enough to glimpse what most everyone else's eyes are already glued to like the finals of "American Idol." "And Creeper," I say. "The guy who kidnapped my daughter."

Beth didn't have a serious wound on her, the doctor told me. Emotionally or physically. And late last night on the telephone, my daughter told me Creeper mostly behaved like a gentleman, only frightened her when he locked her in the car trunk and drowned some kittens.

The trunk thing pisses me off and murdering kittens is so gruesome I don't want to think about it. But maybe my anger at the giant creepola should have limits. He didn't hit, rape, or kill my daughter. Not much to expect of another human being, I suppose, but Creeper being Creeper, I figure the big oaf basically behaved himself.

Jerry, Mr. Diamond, struts and shines between Bluefish and Creeper, the three of them like malevolent cartoon rats—Creeps, Sparkles, and Snake, the boss—parading into some kitchen for a really big cheese heist.

"You'd think making bail, Bluefish would head for places unknown," I say.

"Bluefish is here to see me," Luis says.

I reverse direction again to check my favorite bartender. Luis has been extremely busy since I came in. Barely had time to wave hello and take my order. Glad the fire did so little structural damage he's back raking in the coin already. But someone should tell him all the food tastes like smoke. I don't have the chilies.

"You and Bluefish have an appointment?" I say.

Luis leans across the bar to kiss Gina on the cheek. Gee. Never saw him do that before. To anyone. There's a tenderness in his movements, a vulnerability I've never witnessed. Or am I imagining too much?

"Bluefish and I have unfinished business," Luis says. "I knew only that he would come."

"Me, too," Gina says.

Huh? The combined fragrances of green chili, onion, cilantro, and warming corn tortillas grows overpowering. My forehead pops beads of sweat like I'm being held over a pot of bubbling verde sauce.

"What the hell is going on?" I say.

The two of them stare at me. Luis solemn and resolute. Gina's smile sporting an odd twist.

Why is Gina here, by the way?

FIFTY-SIX

"You are here at a time of awkwardness."

"No kidding, Luis. Your sentence structure is indicative," I say.

"There may be some things, some events, even good friends should not witness or even be aware of," he says.

"Especially good friends," Gina says.

Feels like I'm playing charades. "Say what?"

"The possibility exists one could later be asked questions under oath," Luis says. "And therefore threatened with imprisonment."

"Questions like, did he tell you this, did she say that," Gina says.

Okay. Now I get it. What they're saying is, I don't want to know what the hell is going on.

"It would be better for you to leave," Luis says. "In fact, I have an urgent errand."

I shake my head. "I practically just got here and I'm very hungry." I glance at the menu. "At least give Austin here a little hint. Does this mystery have something to do with Bluefish?"

Luis clasps my shoulder in his right hand. The grip is stern, meant to get my attention. "There is no time. You must take a letter to the post office for me before six o'clock, *por favor.*"

Moving to the cash register, Luis digs beneath the coin tray. What the hell are these two up to? My shoulder thanks me for arranging its release, but warns against further refusal. Luis's fingers pinched me like pliers.

Luis hands me a brown number ten envelope addressed in neatly printed block letters to Rosalinda Sanchez, c/o Teresa Guerrero, 23 Libertad, Zempoala, State of Veracruz, Mexico.

"It is most important," he says. "I trust only you."

BIG MONEY

"Can I have a burrito when I come back?"

Luis smiles. "Umberto will make you something special. Now hurry."

I sigh. Anybody but Luis, I'd tell them to stick the letter. Anxious for my dinner. Gina here beside me. Hells bells, man. Why would I want to leave?

I brush a napkin across my lips and push off my stool.

Luis says, "And please, mi amigo. Do not read the letter."

I stare at him. Gee, pal. That's some level of trust. Imagine Luis thinking I might open his personal, private mail. About to do him a favor, he slaps my face.

I lock the doors of my Camry and rip open the brown envelope. I know, I know. But eight years of stockbrokering withers even an honest man's conscience. With me, Luis's privacy has no shot.

Looks like a letter to his sister. Didn't know he had a sister. And a check for thirty-eight thousand, five-hundred and sixty-four dollars. Nice. Like the envelope, both the check and the letter are for Rosalinda Sanchez.

My Dearest Sister,

It has been ten years since I said goodbye to our small village by the sea. Ten years since I last saw you, Juana, and Esmeralda, my fatherless nieces. Though I long to return home, I cannot. You know as well as I that our family and the village need the American money I send.

Because there is new danger for me here in New Jersey, I would like you to have the money which I have enclosed. Instead of the regular monthly amount, this check represents everything I have saved in the last ten years.

I hope you use at least part of the money to enroll my nieces in a private school where they will learn English well. The money was always for you and their education. The only thing different is that you are to have the money now, in case this danger proves too great a hurdle. Do not be frightened by my words. You know how I tend to dramatize the simplest events.

I must also tell you about a woman I have met. Nothing has been arranged. I have not spoken of my feelings yet. But I believe I have fallen in love.

Ha. I can imagine your smile as you translate this last sentence. Or perhaps Aunt Teresa is reading this letter to you, and the old woman has made you all laugh making her silly voices.

I imagine the whole Guerrero-Sanchez family will be much surprised that I mention my love for a woman. But no one could be more surprised than myself. I did not think myself open to such feelings, especially in America. Yet here I am, your lonely brother, imagining the love a wife and children would offer.

Her name is Angelina, little angel, and though my back was to the door when she first entered my restaurant and my life, I still felt her power, her presence. A tingling at the top of my spine.

Without turning, I knew a great warrior had walked into the room. Imagine my surprise when I saw it was a woman, a mature woman, but with flashing dark hair and shiny bright eyes like the girls from Veracruz. A woman that made my heart beat faster with desire.

Enough. Perhaps one day you will meet her. Who knows what life brings?

Though they must have forgotten by now what I look like, tell Juana and Esmeralda that I love them. And remind them their uncle urgently wishes his nieces to learn English. Until I see you all again, I remain,

Your loving brother, Luis.

FIFTY-SEVEN

The restaurant menu's Spanish descriptions are more helpful than the English. But all Max really knows is that the Mexican food he ate before tasted squishy. Max likes steaks, pork chops, and Jerry's favorite, barbecued ribs. Stuff you chew, not mushy-mush things like refried beans, avocados, and gooey cheese.

"What is hamburguesa?" Max says.

He lifts his gaze, finds Jerry giving him a sideways nod that means to look over the restaurant. He and Jerry already check out this Mexican place, the people inside. Max doesn't see reason to do it again.

"Max," Jerry says.

Bluefish glances at them over his menu.

Max pushes himself out of the booth. Bartender is making drinks. Big blond guy playing with laptop computer. Austin Carr left two minutes ago, not that Max worry about him. In fact, except Mexican behind bar, nobody in whole place looks like they could slow Max down.

Max nods at Jerry that everything is okay, then points at the restroom sign. "Be right back."

His business finished, Max glances at himself in the mirror while washing his hands. That empty feeling grips him again. He sees it in his eyes. The same desolation that unnerved him this afternoon looking at the cloudless sky.

A world without life.

Max reaches inside his new sport coat—Jerry says the old one smelled bad—and removes the Smith & Wesson revolver Jerry gave him to carry this evening. The blue-black steel cools his sweaty palm.

The worry hits Max strong tonight. He hasn't carried his father's arrowhead for luck in two years.

The gun against his hip, Max pushes open the bathroom door with his shoulder and sticks his head out. Nothing. He hurries to the end of the short hallway where he can see the biggest part of the restaurant's bar area. Nothing wrong there. Everything look the same.

Holding the Smith & Wesson mostly in his coat pocket, Max strolls through doorway, then stops in main dining room where he can see both Bluefish and Jerry.

Trouble. A uniformed policeman stands beside Bluefish, a pen and leather-bound ticket pad in his hands. The cop talking to Jerry. Shifting his weight from one foot to the other. Back and forth. Back and forth. Glancing now over his shoulder at Max.

Why is cop so nervous?

Max hurries forward, his thumb sliding back the revolver's hammer.

A woman to his right glimpses Max's gun. She gasps, then points at it for her friend, another middle-aged woman. The second one screams.

The three explosions come closely together. Max hears them as one long stuttering peel of thunder, a tornado rolling over him from behind. But each bullet feels different, separate from the sound and separate from each other. First bullet burns his back like fire. The second knocks all air from his lungs. Third bullet taps his shoulder like the hand of a small child.

On his way to restaurant's wood floor, sliding down like a melting snowman, Max watches the nervous policeman draw his weapon and fire two shots, one each into the heads of Bluefish and Jerry.

Max's weapon tumbles away as he hits the floor. So quick. Everything happen so fast.

He tries to stand, but Max's legs don't work anymore. His hands push okay, and he can slightly raise his head.

Big blond guy in shorts and blue T-shirt stand over him now, a wisp of gray smoke rising from barrel of small-caliber handgun. Stinky little twenty-two. Hit man special, Jerry once say. Bullet bounce around inside skull.

Max watches the blond guy aim the little gun at Max's head. He remembers the morning's tasteless air. That cloudless sky.

A world without life.

FIFTY-EIGHT

Still in my Camry, I read Luis's letter for the third time. Is he talking about Gina? Angelina Farascio? He can't be in love with the other Angelina I know, Angelina Bonacelli, although in my mind, Mama Bones definitely approaches warrior-like status.

If Luis's love interest is Gina Farascio, that would explain why he kissed her so tenderly in the bar a few minutes ago, maybe why she was at Luis's to begin with. That little peck on the cheek was the deepest display of affection I've ever seen from my favorite bartender. Luis in love. Why the idea almost—

A truck or bus backfires in spurts. Kinda like a TV cop-show shootout. Bam-bam-bam...bam-bam...bam.

Wait a minute. I forgot the Camry's windows are rolled up, the engine already purring. It's possible I may have failed to appreciate the true, more violent nature of those recurring bam-bams.

Rolling down the car window, I recognize another sound now—human adults screaming and yelling their bloody heads off—and even Austin Carr can put bam-bam and eek-eek together. Gunshots.

I hop my ass out of the Camry.

Oops. Luis's letter tumbles from my lap. Don't want to be running back inside with that little flag unfurled. Show Luis my true, villainous nature.

I fold Rosalinda's check inside the letter, tuck everything under the Camry's driver's seat. My car's semi-shag rug is a litter box of rice-sized pebbles and coarse beach sand.

An orange sun fades below the parking lot's pine tree border as I jog between a crowd of cars and SUVs. Branchtown lies in growing shadow. Small birds cheep-cheep their goodbyes to the safety of daylight. Tires and engines hum along Highway 35, a thick steel river of Friday night traffic.

Two uniformed Branchtown cops burst out of Luis's Mexican Grill. I view mostly backsides as they run across my path, then dodge screeching rubber and two-ton fenders crossing the highway. They must be chasing somebody.

I look left, then right. Whoever they're chasing—maybe the shooter?—he's doing a great job of camouflage. Can't see anyone they could be running after. And I notice the cops haven't drawn their guns.

Maybe they're chasing dick.

"I hope to hell you got a decent look at them," Franny says. Her green eyes are dead-set against me.

How the hell was I supposed to know the cops were the shooters? "I can tell you something about them."

El Capitan Frances Chapman and her sidekick, Chef Stuart, arrived at Luis's eighteen minutes after the gunplay, twelve minutes behind the paramedics and a Branchtown patrol car.

"Well?"

"Two white males, dressed as Branchtown policemen," I say. "One of them was one-sixty to one-seventy-five pounds, forty to forty-five years old. The other was two hundred pounds or more, in his twenties. Both of them five-ten to six-feet tall. Didn't get hair color because of the police hats. No visible scars or tattoos."

Once again, watching TV cop shows makes the witness invaluable to law enforcement investigators. Thank you, Detective Andy Sipowicz.

Franny says to Stuart, "You getting this?"

Everybody in the place is working pen on paper. First thing when they got there, after securing half the restaurant with crime scene tape, the real Branchtown cops told Luis's patrons to sit down, write their name, address, and phone number on paper. I know it helped calm the place. The tears and shrieking lost most of their momentum as people tried to remember how to spell Smith and Jones.

Franny saying, "Think you'd recognize these two if you saw them again?"

"Maybe," I say. My eyes took a few decent profile shots. "Maybe not."

"Come on, then." Franny turns me over to a uniformed trooper the size of Paul Bunyan. Or maybe Bunyan's blue ox. His hands feel like horns, and he uses his state trooper chest belt to bump me around like livestock. Franny saying, "Let's have you look at some mug shots."

Moving toward a joint exit with Trooper Bunyan, I seem to have lost weight. About a hundred pounds. My toes fly across Luis's hardwood floor. At least I'm on my feet. Barely breathing, Creeper went out on a stretcher. Multiple gunshot wounds, including one to the head. Kinda' harsh punishment for locking my daughter Beth in a car trunk.

Bluefish and Jerry will leave later. In rubber body bags.

"It's a simple question, Carr," Franny says two hours later. "Did you see Gina Farascio near Bluefish, either before or after the shooting?"

"I'm tired," I say. "I want to go home."

"Okay. As soon as you tell me what I want to know. Now how about it? Did you see Gina beside Bluefish?"

I sigh. My back is killing me. First the barstool, then the back seat of a cruiser, now this spine-twisting chair at Trooper Interrogation Central. I wonder if I've been transported to a former Soviet bloc country so they can torture me.

Having witnessed two men's brains oozing across the restaurant floor, all that fresh, salty-smelling blood, I couldn't see what direction we were headed, let alone where we ended up. I can't even say how long a ride it was.

Where's Chef Stuart with the fresh coffee?

"Gina checked Bluefish's pulse. That's what she was doing as I came back inside," I say.

Franny's eyes narrow. "She was crouched beside him?"

"Yeah. Touching his neck."

"Which hand?"

"I don't remember."

Franny leans forward so that our faces are six inches apart. "Think. It's important. Was she reaching across his chest?"

"Why?"

"It just is. Think. What was she doing with her hands?"

"Is something missing from Bluefish's body?"

"Shut up. Did you—"

"See, I ask because the only person I saw going through Bluefish's pockets was you, Franny."

"Captain Chapman to you."

"Captain, my ass."

Just for a second, Ms. Strawberry shows up on El Capitan's face. One of her sea-green eyes winks at me. "You had your chance."

FIFTY-NINE

Max is a soft, helium-filled circus balloon. He floats and bounces along the operating room's white-tile ceiling. Below him, blue doctors and green nurses huddle in an egg-shaped circle around his naked body.

How is this? Max is two places at one time.

Max is conscious of a danger, aware that being separated from his flesh means his spirit or his mind could get lost. But he is not that much afraid. There is a sturdy string attached to that helium-filled balloon, and whenever he wants, Max can will himself down the line, like fireman down a pole to the operating table.

Max knows this for sure, somehow, and also, he likes this floating. On a big screen in a corner of the operating room, he can see memories like movies. Or at least this one memory. The one playing now—how Max hid as a child and waited under the cages to kill his Mama's new husband. How the smell of the cats made him sick. And how he endured by imagining himself feeding the lion tamer to lion tamer's own lions. The same smelly cats that ate his father.

But at the scene where Max is ready to strike, ready to kill the lion tamer, the lions jump through the movie screen and claw Max's back.

He screams in shock and pain.

Max can't open his eyes, and he can't move his hands. Maybe this is dream, too. Or maybe now Max is dead. Those blue doctors or the lion killed him.

"We could write an article for the *New England Medical Journal* on this man's head," a woman says.

Max's mouth and throat are sore like he swallowed a basketball. And someone must have hit him on the head with a big hammer and then left the handle sticking out. Each heartbeat brings a new throb of hurt to the top and back of his skull.

"The bullet must have struck at an incredibly lucky angle," a man's voice says.

Max hears people speaking, such soft voices talking about him, the hospital patient Max Zakowsky, but it is probably a dream. Like floating above his body and remembering the smell of the cats.

Gentle fingers probe the base of Max's skull.

"No, feel that," the woman says.

Max wishes he could see her. Her voice is like classical music.

"I'll bet this man's sphenoid bone is at least fifty percent thicker than yours or mine," she says.

Maybe this is not a dream. Max never hear of a sphenoid bone before this moment. How could he imagine it?

"I hope you never get a chance to compare, Sydney, but I know this man was damn lucky with the other three bullets. No bones, major arteries, or organs were damaged. He'll be walking out of here in a week."

Max opens his eyes. He wasn't dreaming. There is man and woman doctors standing beside his bed.

"Quicker even," Max says.

Intense, burning orange light becomes the early morning sun shining in Max's window. Is his mind floating again?

No, Max is waking up in a hospital bed, the searing pain from his head to his hip no longer part of a dream. The pain is real. Hard to believe bullets could deliver so much hurt but not kill him.

Assassins.

Sitting up feels impossible. His body seems broken inside, muscles and bones unable to work together. Mind fuzzy with pain and something else...drugs probably. At least he can see now, move his hands and feet, legs if he wants.

Max rings a bell for the nurse.

A gray-haired woman with two sofa pillows for a chest and one major ass walks into his room ten minutes later.

"Where pants?" Max says.

"Only when I have to," woman says. "Right now, I'm running full commando."

Max knows she is being silly although he doesn't understand the joke. A sense of humor is good thing. Those huge breasts look pretty good, too.

"Your clothes, what's left of them, are in the closet, Mr. Zakowsky. But don't think you're going anywhere."

Max tries to smile. "Max not going anywhere today. But would like to see my blue jeans."

The nurse brings him a shredded mess. The other nurse, the skinny one with thin hair, explained how the ambulance guys cut up his shirt and pants to save him.

The woman with big ass and big tits stays close to the bed after she hands him his clothes. Close enough to touch if he wanted.

"What are you lookin' for, honey?"she says.

Kneading the fabric carefully with his fingers, Max finds the spear tip with his thumb and forefinger. His father was right. There must be a spirit in the rock that protects its wearer from assassins.

The next day, Mama Bones says, "What did the coppers want?"

"If I know who did this," Max says. "Also if I recognize anyone. If I willing to look at books of photos."

Max sits up, grateful that his pain is fading, but tired from walking up and down the hospital hall all day. Mama Bones could be the new boss of Bluefish's family, however, and Max knows Jerry would tell him to show the old hag respect.

"What did you say to them?" Mama Bones says.

"Nothing. I learn more from them than they learn from me."

"Yeah? So you know Bluefish and your friend Jerry are dead?"

"I see their brains. Yes."

Mama Bones nods. "Nunzio says it notta him. But my niece Gina, Tony Farascio's wife, she was at the bar when you and Bluefish got shot. She tells me she has nothing to do with killing, but I'm not so sure. She was very mad about Tony. And was also mad about Anne Marie."

"Anne? Why?"

"Gina was Anne Marie's friend. I think. Once."

So. That's it. Max finally understand. Anne. Frances. And Gina. All three of them.

Maybe Max have his own suspect now for Anne Marie's murder. He needs to check something, but if Max is right, he will kill her. Kill woman who kill his Anne, along with Austin Carr and Mexican bartender for shooting Jerry.

Assassins.

Maybe Max drown them all together in bag like smelly little cats.

SIXTY

The telephone pressed against my ear, I slide gently onto my living room couch, ease back, and stretch my feet out.

Some beatings I like to take lying down.

I just spent an exhausting and stress-filled Saturday morning reading the newspaper. The kids' mutual funds are down, my horoscope sucks, and the local rag whose name I won't mention ran another follow-up on Shore and Bluefish. Plus, I have a sinister premonition about this call I've been trying to make.

"May I help you?" the operator says.

"I'm having trouble reaching a number." I rattle off the seven digits of Susan's house line. My old ranchero. I don't like numbers much, my business being so full of them. And I can't remember my morning routine when I lived there, or even what Susan looked like naked. But this damn phone number is burned into my head like some ancient petroglyph into rock. 555-5443.

"The line's been disconnected, sir."

A hole in the earth opens up beneath my couch. I'm plunging through space like Dorothy in *The Wizard of Oz*. "Are you sure? That's been my house line for eight years."

"That number was disconnected yesterday, sir. By the billing party."

I park in front of the old homestead and immediately know the truth. The realtor's FOR SALE sign stuck in the lawn pretty much tells the tale.

Jesus. I can't believe Susan would do this.

Dazed, I stumble inside the house through an unlocked back door, inspect the empty rooms and cupboards, the bare walls and floors. Vacant spaces where I played Legos with Beth and Ryan. Barren corners once stacked with toys.

My gut winces, as if claws were ripping my flesh.

The telephone rings as I unlock my apartment twenty minutes later. The shrill clanging echoes in the empty living room. I hurry, hoping for no logical reason it's the kids. Did I leave that kitchen light on?

"Hello?"

"Hey, pal, it's Walter. How you been?"

I sigh. "Fabulous. Susan and the kids moved without telling me."

"Sorry," he says. "I just wanted to let you know I signed those papers you sent me and had them notarized. I dropped them off at the post office on my way into work this morning."

I don't think Walter is even slightly interested Susan skipped out. Maybe he's right. Why should he be?

"A hitter like you, dialing for dollars on a Saturday?" Busting balls is what Walter deserves.

"Yeah, well I'm still working on getting all my Shore people over," he says. "Thought this might be a good day to remind them how well I've managed their money."

A month ago I considered him a friend. Now he's calling up my customers and telling them their money's at risk with Shore. "Right, Walter. And the follow-up story on Bluefish and Shore Securities today had nothing at all to do with your decision. Are you going to send our customers reprints?"

"Hey, that's a great idea."

I must be the world's dumbest victim. I can't believe I just said that. "Well, thanks for signing those papers, Walter. Nice doing business with you."

"When do I get my first check?" he says.

"I'm not sure. Call the escrow company where you sent the papers. I can't see where it would take them more than one or two business days."

"All right," he says. "Take it easy."

"Later, Walter."

I wonder if Rags has received his paperwork yet, if he'll sign as easily as Walter. Carr's Famous Plan to Create Opportunity from Crisis proceeds nicely on course. I'm not planning on hitting The Fortune 500. Honestly, it's mostly payback, although I would hope one day to cinch myself enough moolah to secure Beth's and Ryan's college education. It's possible.

But my thoughts won't stay on business. The sight of my empty old ranchero, that ugly FOR SALE sign...the memories there with my kids. These images just won't stay out of my head but minutes at a time.

The Creeper only took Beth. Susan kidnapped both my children.

SIXTY-ONE

The telephone wakes me just before midnight. I'm stretched out on my couch with the TV on, Sipowicz once again putting the screws to some scumbag fink. Although now that I think about it, I have quite a little career blooming myself as a law enforcement snitch.

Reaching over my head for the living room phone, I remember Susan's skipped with the kids. Maybe the caller is Beth or Ryan, ratting out their overprotective mother. Probably wishful thinking, but my kids love me. I know that. They're going to want to see their pop.

"Hello?" I say.

Click. A hang up.

Must be a wrong number, the caller probably expecting a female voice on this end. You'd think this late, even on a Saturday night, people using the telephone would take a bit more care pressing buttons.

I rest the phone in its cradle and return my head to its well-worn spot on the padded arm rest. A commercial's running instead of my favorite cop show, and my eyes slowly shut. I'm thinking maybe I should make my way to the bedroom, take my clothes off, when the damn phone rings again.

Ass-a-hola.

I pick up. "Hello?"

Click. Another hang-up.

Gee. And I tried to sound so vibrant and appealing that time. Now I'm pissed.

Okay, this is why I ordered the full complement of new technology on my apartment telephone. I sit up on the couch and flip on the table lamp, dial star-six-nine. Takes nine or ten rings, but finally an elderly man picks up and growls hello. Sounds like a lifetime smoker of unfiltered tree trunks.

"Did you just call 555-6564?" I say.

"Nope. This is a pay phone in Clooneys. I was walking by."

"Did you see who was just using the phone?"

Silence. One beat...two. The old geezer's probably trying to remember what phone I'm talking about. "A woman," he says.

"Really? What did she look like?"

Silence. Then another voice whispering in the background. "I don't know," he says finally, "but I gotta go. Doris is waiting for me."

He hangs up.

Think I just got my first senior discount.

Walking into Clooneys forty minutes later, checking the bar, the first thing my peepers latch onto is State Trooper Frances Dahler Chapman, El Cap-i-tan herself. She's alone and deep into the martinis, I'm guessing. She's hunched over the bar, the strawberry-blonde hair slightly askew, in a black sleeveless dress. As I'm standing in the entrance area staring, she lights a cigarette with wobbly hands.

Franny's drunk. Oh, boy.

Wonder if it was Franny that called me? I don't see anybody else here I know, but there's no real evidence she or anyone else I know was the caller. Big coincidence I get a phone call from my second-favorite bar and restaurant, but it could have been just a wrong number.

I choose to ignore other, less sexually promising possibilities, however. I focus instead on the memory of Franny's naked body in bed with me.

"I don't want to talk to you," Franny says. "You lied to me. You lied to the Grand Jury."

"I had to. Bluefish said he'd kill my children."

Franny glances at me sidesaddle. Her lime-colored eyes radiate the glassy quality of calm water. "I could have protected them," she says.

I shake my head. "No way. You could have locked me up, maybe made me safe. I totally would have done what you wanted if I didn't have kids. But I can't have them pulled out of school, hidden away someplace. Frightened."

Franny slurps at her half-done martini. The sound attracts the glance of Clooneys young bartender, a crew cut athletic type who wasn't all that pleased to take my drink order. Probably figured he was going to pick up Franny's disassembled but luscious pieces when Clooneys shuts the doors at one-thirty.

God, aren't men awful?

Franny sighs. Her moist gaze locks with mine. "Maybe you were right. I should have realized what you were up against," she says. "And the truth is, it was Fluebish I wanted. Now that he's dead, I think I'm not so mad at you anymore."

Fluebish? The lady is bombed. I'm starting to worry a little. She might be too drunk. I mean, even stockbrokers have pride. You can't go around humping the unconscious. That's like selling limited partnerships to your mother.

"You're not going to prosecute me?" I say.

"Probably not. The investigation is over."

I think I like the sound of this. "What about Talbot's murder?"

"That's almost done, too," she says. "We traced the video recording equipment to a stolen trunk of stuff that matched swag found in Bluefish's warehouse. Bluefish or a friend of his must have killed her."

"So there really was a DVD of the murder?"

"I think so," she says. "But no one will ever see it again."

"Why?"

Franny gazes out Clooneys giant bar window at the dark Atlantic. "Because the killer was powerful enough to make it disappear."

"Powerful enough to push around cops?"

Her gaze finds me again. She blinks. "Yup. Mallory for sure. Maybe his chief. Branchtown's a cesspool. The cocal lops are protecting someone."

"I don't believe you."

Franny finishes her see-through. I'm guessing number four or five by the slump of her shoulders. She giggles. "Cocal lops? How can you even understand me?"

SIXTY-TWO

Franny laps at her last-call martini like a thirsty Labrador. "Ever see that old Jack Nicholson movie *Chinatown?*" she says.

"Not more than twenty times," I say. "I think Robert Townsend won an Oscar for it."

"Who's Robert Townsend?"

"He wrote it. An original screenplay."

"Oh. Well, then," she says, "you'll know exactly what I'm talking about. They, I mean he, repeats the line a bunch of times in different parts of the movie. 'It's Chinatown, Jake,' like there's nothing Jake can do, things are unknowable in that part of the city."

"Townsend was writing about the dark side of people's souls, not geography," I say. "You never know what goes on inside a person's heart."

"Exactly," she says. "That's what I mean. You wouldn't believe what goes on between powerful friends in New Jersey, Austin. You really wouldn't."

"What are you talking about?"

Franny sets down her martini glass and stares out Clooneys dark bay windows again at the invisible sea. "Me, Austin. I'm talking about me."

Ms. Strawberry bows her head and begins to weep, eventually hugging me for emotional support. Perhaps persuaded by the electrifying sensation of Franny's breasts pressed against my abdomen, I decide information-pumping time is over. I mean, I have no idea what the hell she's talking about.

Chinatown?

I work on something clever to say in hopes of facilitating the switch from pump to hump. Then I remember the pervasive Austin Carr tendency to overemphasize verbal intercourse.

Show her how you feel, Ace, don't tell her.

I slide my hand around Franny's waist, pull her across the space between our barstools, then bend down to kiss her. She doesn't turn away, and our lips come together like pancakes and maple syrup. Tender at first, I let my passion build until our tongues are doing a slow wet tango.

When the kiss over, my mouth is numb and Franny's whole body is relaxed against me. She tilts her head up and whispers. "Wanna follow me home?"

I kiss her neck. "I might be persuaded."

The bar check has been paid, including a nice tip for the disappointed bartender. Franny's stuffing a lighter and a pack of Marlboros into her purse. Big Daddy's revving up with thoughts of a midnight ride.

"Listen," she says, "I sorgot fumthing. Be a nice Austin and go wait for me in the parking lot, or take a pee, will you? I have to talk to someone."

Huh? Where did this come from? And who the hell is she going to talk to. There's only one table left in the dining area. No customers in the bar but us and one older man. "I'm not allowed to meet them?"

"He's very shy."

"He?"

"A trooper friend. I have a subpoena for him in my purse. Now go pee, or wash your face, or wait for me outside. I just need a couple of minutes."

I glance at the geezer across the bar. If he's getting paid by the State Troopers, it's a pension. "He's already here?"

"Yes. Now give me five minutes of privacy. Please?"

Curiosity rules this stockbroker's heart, and when I leave Franny in the sunken bar area, duck out Clooneys entrance, I make a sharp left turn instead of heading for my parked Camry.

The restaurant's beach front lights are off because the deck's still closed this time of year, so when I slip around the building, stand in front of the big bay window and stare unseen into the lighted restaurant, I can see Clooneys last customers talking at a table and Franny in the bar like I'm watching television. For the first time, I notice the very late, lingering diners. One of them is Vick's daughter, Carmela Bonacelli.

My gaze slides back to Franny. She's digging in her black purse, doesn't see the person walking up from behind until the new arrival takes my empty stool. The familiar woman has large dark eyes, long black hair, and like Franny, also wears a black, sleeveless, scooped-neck dress.

What the hell is Gina doing here?

Side by side, Franny and Gina look like onyx salt and pepper shakers. My spiciest dream.

When Franny finally sees her, there's no surprise. She and Gina seem much more disturbed by the similarity of their dresses.

Slowly, like she really really hates to give it up, might even take it back, Franny pulls a small thin package from her purse and hands it to Gina.

Could it be?

SIXTY-THREE

Pressing his back against the wall, Max slides down on his haunches to wedge himself into a dark corner. Make himself as small as possible; hard to see, but coiled and ready. Max is able to jump out quickly like a spider.

Max takes three long, slow, deep breaths, trying to clear his mind of thoughts. He may have to hold this uncomfortable position for many hours, maybe all night. Is best to relax.

When he first started working for Bluefish, Max used a more direct manner. He would walk right up to the mark, tell him his time was up, or maybe knock the man down first, then talk. Most of the time, the mark would let Max do whatever Max was supposed to do. Beat the mark up, break a bone. But sometimes the mark would run, and Max hated those chases. Max is too big to run fast for long, plus things always seemed to get in his way. Couches. Cars. Other people. By the time he caught the mark, Max was usually too pissed to hold back. Twice he killed the mark when he was not supposed to. Also, once or twice, maybe three times now counting that Mexican bartender, the mark actually got away.

Make Max look bad.

Max takes another series of long, slow, deep breaths. His body relaxes, gravity working him even lower into the corner. Experience has taught Max to hide and relax. Guarantee himself the element of surprise, make his first move very strong. Get your hands on him before mark knows he's not alone.

And once Max got his hands on someone...

SIXTY-FOUR

Her two-story house ranks as ancient so it's no surprise the original pine floorboards creak. But do I detect a certain rhythm...like footsteps?

I sit back on the blood red living room sofa and hold my breath to listen. A grandfather clock tick-tocks in the foyer. The oil-burning basement heater pops and rumbles. And yes, there...bare or stocking feet pad gently toward me down the hall.

I stuff the DVD under my laptop and work hard to put on my three-o'clock-in-the-morning, full-boat Carr grin. Not exactly a simple trick. And definitely not sincere. I mean, how am I supposed to be calm and forthright when this DVD suggests last night's love interest may not be the innocent beauty I imagined?

Clever of me to wake her up.

I gasp when she steps into the living room light. Oh, my. And oops. Oh my, because Gina's wearing nothing but white athletic socks. And oops because she's using both hands and all ten red-nailed fingers to grasp a pump-action, single-barrel shotgun.

"You found the DVD, didn't you?" Gina says.

"DVD?" If it wasn't for acronyms, I'd be pretty much speechless. My gaze is tightly focused on her bare breasts and that shotgun in the same close-up. Visually and emotionally, it's a lot to absorb.

Gina's slender right foot slides back, toes out. Improving her balance.

"I know you found it," she says. "Wrapped in my black dress."

My lips move without sound. Maybe my throat's choked with fear, but I'd rather think I'm distracted by the long curve of Ms.

Shotgun's hip, the loose weight of her breasts swinging below the carved gun stock.

Watch me get a boner.

"I just checked the bathroom," Gina says. "You rifled the hamper, found the black dress. So...you've got my DVD."

I take a long, deep breath. On tough stock and bond clients, this often works as a show of calm sincerity. "I swear I don't know what you're talking about."

Gina racks a shell into the firing chamber.

Guess my pledge of innocence lacked conviction.

I lift my iBook and offer her the DVD. My heart ticks to an even quicker time. My ego slips a notch. Time was, the full-boat Carr grin and a reasonable lie got me over these bumpy spots with naked women.

I probably don't have to worry anymore about that boner.

"Play it," Gina says. "We'll solve the murder together."

I slide the disk into my Mac and wonder if I'm really going to view what the *Branchtown Sun* calls the "MISSING HOTEL MURDER VIDEO."

The DVD's first images show a thirty-ish woman primping her hair before a gilded oval mirror.

"Don't you want to fast-forward?" Gina says. "Get right to the choking and burning?"

On screen, the victim cracks open her hotel room door. My jaw drops as Gina's digital image rushes inside, pushing right through the startled hotel guest and knocking her flat on the carpet.

I turn from the laptop. "So it was you."

Gina raises the pump-action level with my nose. "Watch the video."

I suck an extended breath. Instead of blowing my head off right now, Gina apparently needs a short refresher course in homicide. Okay. Take your time, dear. In fact, I don't mind studying the course material, too, maybe even take a little Q&A afterward.

Or write a five-hundred page essay.

On my computer screen, Gina's image finally stops kicking a motionless Anne Marie Talbot. And I do mean finally. Must have taken Gina at least five minutes to release all her jealousy, her sense of betrayal.

It was an outburst of rage and fury I haven't witnessed since I wouldn't eat Susan's pimento casserole.

Oh, my. Maybe Gina's not quite satisfied. (
Shotgun throws her knee onto Talbot's chest. Her ha
Anne Marie's throat, the throttling action energized
forward. Transferring her weight.

My belly rolls and crashes like ocean backwash. This is worse
than ugly. I'm watching a real murder.

On screen, Gina's image hops through the sliding glass door onto
Talbot's hotel-room balcony. She comes back seconds later carrying a
small hibachi, one of those Japanese-style cast-iron grillers. The
barbecue coals already glow white hot.

Watching this video, I'm panting like Lamaze class, trying to
keep my stomach right side up. I'm thinking the hibachi was never
mentioned in the newspapers, but I must have been subconsciously
wondering since Franny showed me the autopsy report. I remember
asking myself what a "charcoal burner" was doing in Talbot's hotel
room. Sounds like a basic and serious violation of fire codes, not to
mention common logic.

"Franny was having a barbecue?" I say.

Gina gazes intently at her own image on the computer screen.
"Steaks for her and my husband. Although Tony didn't stick around
for dinner."

I suppose my plan is to delay Gina for as long as I can, pray for
the cavalry.

"Tony knew he was going to see her that evening? And you
followed him to the Martha Washington?" I say.

"Yup. I heard them humping through the door, then fighting
over whether or not he should stay. When Tony left her room, I hid
so he wouldn't see me, then went back. You should have seen her
face when she saw it was me, not Tony changing his mind about
dinner."

"Jealous rage, huh?"

"Anne Marie and I are old friends. Screwing my husband was a
really shitty thing to do."

I feel my forehead bunch into a wrinkled mess. "Old friends?
You mean that story you told me about Franny being a mob party
girl with Ann Marie was really your story? It was you and Ann

Marie?"

"All three of us," Gina says. "The Poker Pals, Tony and his guys called us. We were popular. Serving drinks. Bathroom blow jobs. For years and years, even after a couple of us tried marriage. Tony's guys knew us so well, trusted us, one night they decided all three of us should get jobs aiding and abetting Tony's businesses. Later, he rented our services to other...organizations."

"Ingenious," I say. "Worthy of Arthur Conan Doyle, a Moriarty scheme. Anne Marie took accounting classes, earned her C.P.A. and went to work for the A.A.S.D. Franny went with the New Jersey State Troopers. But how about you, Gina? Where did you hook up?"

Her mouth twists into something only resembling a smile. "Tony decided I'd be best suited for something else."

"Like what?"

Gina's finger slides back to the shotgun's trigger. "Keep asking questions, you might find out."

"You're a hit-man—I mean, hit-woman?"

Gina shrugs. "More odd jobs than anything else. A little procurement, or carrying weapons into places men can't. Once and a while I surprise people who need surprising. Sometimes a combination."

I need to line up an inventory of questions like icy bombs for a snowball fight. Keep 'em coming. Although I still can't figure exactly which cavalry's going to ride to my rescue.

"Where did the DVD come from?" I say. "How did Franny get it?"

"I'm tired of the questions. Stand up."

"Oh, come on, Gina. What's your hurry? Who was bugging Anne Marie's room?"

Her big almond-shaped eyes stare at me. She shrugs. "Bluefish put in the recording equipment. Talbot was working for him. They were hoping to catch you in there humping her."

"But I'm single."

"Yeah, but she's an A.A.S.D. official investigating your firm. The potential scandal would've made you think about cooperating."

"So after the murder, Franny got the DVD from who—Detective Mallory?"

Gina smiles. "Whom..."

I shrug.

"I don't know," she says. "Mallory, or Bluefish. I just told her to get it for me."

I'm almost out of snowballs. "But wasn't Franny working for Bluefish? Pretending to be after him, indicting him, but really setting it all up so he'd be acquitted? Why would she give you the DVD?"

"With Bluefish dead, she didn't have many options. Franny and Anne Marie were always freelance, this time working for Bluefish. I work for Tony's family. My family. They're the kind of people Franny knows she can't refuse. Especially with Bluefish gone."

Gina pushes the shotgun closer to my face. "Now stand up. We're going to walk slowly through the kitchen and then down into the basement. I need you to help me carry something upstairs."

I shake my head. "You mean that shotgun's too messy to use in the living room."

She shows me a real smile this time. Nasty and cold, but real. "Stand up."

I stagger to my feet and head for her kitchen. I can walk but I can't swallow.

There's a live boa around my neck.

SIXTY-FIVE

Maybe I perused too much Carlos Castaneda-type mysticism in my youth, but all I can think about on my way down Gina's basement steps: This could be my Last Battle on Earth. I must give these moments the attention my life's purpose deserves. I try to absorb every detail of my surroundings, let loose my inner warrior's imagination for fight or flight.

Too bad I don't have any peyote.

I also wish I could remember how that Don Juan shaman character created a double. Boy, would I like to be somewhere else.

"Take it slow," Gina says.

She's four or five steps behind me on the basement stairs, yet I can feel that shotgun aimed at my back. The weapon's like a glowing poker radiating red-hot death.

I mean, Gina's definitely going to kill me. I've seen the DVD, asked way too many questions, because as we all know, those of us with the Gift of Gab never know when to shut the hell up. It's a universal fact.

I nearly choke over my next assertion. "I can keep my mouth shut, Gina. You don't have to kill me."

"It won't hurt," she says. "I'll make it a head shot."

Ringo is playing the drums of my heart. Back-beat, jump-beat, downbeat. Everything, all at once. My ribs stretch from the inside.

As I approach the bottom of the basement stairs, Gina flips a switch, and an overhead light pops on. Dark-stained wood shelves cover the cement basement walls. Typical garage and basement junk fills the carefully organized shelf space. Beach chairs. Lawn food. Stacks of clay gardening pots. Broken exercise equipment. Discards of suburban life on the Jersey Shore. About head-high, a narrow strip of double-thick window shows the moonlight outside and last summer's dead marigolds.

"If I let you live, I'd always worry you'd hurt me with the information," Gina says. "Or somebody like Franny Chapman would make you talk to save their own ass. I'm sorry, sweetie. You're a pretty good fuck. But I just can't take the chance, or the stress."

"Then why did you bring me home with you last night?" I say. "Why even let me have the chance of finding that DVD?"

"When you came back in Clooneys last night, I knew you'd seen Franny give me that DVD. I had to find out how badly you wanted to watch it, if you knew what it was. Besides, I enjoyed taking you away from her."

Other than folding Gina up in one of those collapsible aluminum beach chairs, I see nothing in this basement that could help me take away that shotgun. I see nothing, that is, until I spin around to face her.

Oh. My. God. Creeper. He's balled up like a spider beneath the basement stairway. An electric shock jolts my spine.

In the spilt second I debate whether I should speak, leap, or do nothing, Creeper grabs the initiative. Any action on my part now is suddenly too late.

As her white-stocking foot touches the last step, Creeper grabs Gina by the ankle, dumps the naked, dark-haired beauty onto the basement floor.

Ka-boom. The shotgun goes off. Blue fire flashes from the muzzle. Stacks of burnt-orange clay flower pots explode just inches from my left hip. A cloud of smoke rises toward me from the basement floor.

My ears buzz from the blast. Shards of clay flower pot splash against my pants and shoes as Creeper pounces from behind the stairway. Two blurry-fast steps and he has Gina by the head and shoulders. I hear Gina's neck snap like a broomstick as I lunge for her shotgun.

Ordinarily, I'd stop, take a moment, say a few words about Gina's fine character. But hey, and I figure she'd understand better than anyone, I need to focus right now on staying alive.

At the conclusion of my dive, my chest slams the basement

floor. But my outstretched fingers find and grab the shotgun. I roll hard to the right, trying to give myself some distance, but Creeper's on me like a cave-in. His forearms press my head and shoulders flat against the cold cement. His hands encircle my throat. The shotgun blast still echoes in my head. The sulfuric odor of burnt gunpowder fills my nose.

The way I figure it, Austin Carr will be a full-boat dead man in two-to-three seconds, soon as Creeper breaks—what did that autopsy report call it—my hyoid bone?

The fingers of my right hand still touch the shotgun, but Creeper's left forearm has my reach pinned to the cement floor. I can barely wiggle my wrist, let alone grip the weapon. But this is my Last Battle on Earth, and I'm about to lose, about to pass on to that other world, that Great Mystery about which we poor humans know so little and worry so much.

Gotta try something, Ace.

Maybe I can twirl the shotgun a little with my wrist and fingers, reposition the barrel so the muzzle's aiming at Creeper's knee and leg. Give him a kiss he won't forget. Yes. There. Like playing spin the bottle.

Creeper's weight presses on me like a stack of marble tombstones. I feel myself blacking out.

Finally, my thumb finds the trigger.

SIXTY-SIX

When my thumb squeezes the trigger, nothing happens. Well, that figures. The shotgun must be jammed. A final, very bad piece of luck for ol' Austin Carr.

I try once more, a near-death panic pushing my actions, giving me a miraculous surge of will. Still nothing. No explosion. And this time my furious attempt to fire the weapon makes the gun stock bounce and rattle on the basement's cement floor.

Creeper's gaze snaps toward the noise.

Well, gee, this is beginning to look like The End. The oft-forecast demise of Austin Carr and his full-boat smile. The semi-orphanization of one Elizabeth Carr and Ryan Carr, two school-age children who—

Air rushes into my desperate lungs. Oh, my. Creeper has decided he'd rather have his paws on the shotgun than around my throat. What a strange tactical decision, especially considering the shotgun so recently proved unreliable. Hell, I was almost unconscious. Go figure.

Creeper's poor judgment not only means oxygen for my air-starved lungs, but now that I can breathe, perhaps I can even launch a counterattack, wrestle free of Creeper's awesome weight.

I throw my shoulders and hips to the left, away from the shotgun. I catch Creeper leaning, his arm reaching for the shotgun. The jerky twist indeed breaks me loose like a stuck jar of peanut butter.

My newly reacquired air supply suddenly tastes even sweeter. A shot of confidence joins the adrenaline zooming through my blood. Kinda like last night at Clooneys when Gina told Franny I'd be spending the night in Brooklyn.

Are you watching, Don Juan? Witnessing this dramatic reversal of my Last Battle on Earth?

I scramble onto my haunches and face Creeper. He's sitting ass-flat on the basement floor, the shotgun between his ox-like thighs. We can't be more than five feet apart. My gaze looks straight down the shotgun's barrel. Talk about evil eyes.

"That gun's jammed," I say.

Though even a broken weapon is disconcerting at this proximity and angle—that black hole smells like eternity—my tone carries a certain hint of superiority. I mean, I pulled that shotgun's trigger. It didn't work. It's not like I'm bluffing.

Why is he smiling?

"Gun not jammed," Creeper says. "No shells in chamber. You have to do this each time."

He works the shotgun's pump. Clickity-clack.

I knew that.

The basement's tomblike silence wraps around me like a shroud.

Employing Gina's pump-action like a conductor's baton, Ludwig van Creeptoven orchestrates me up the basement steps, into the kitchen, and then into Gina's side yard through a screened kitchen door and wooden back stairs.

On my left is a one-car garage shaped like a mausoleum. On my right, parked in Gina's hosta and rock-lined cement driveway, a black Buick LeSabre waits for us like a hearse. The excited chatter of morning birdcalls emanates from the evergreens that separate Gina from her neighbors.

I love that I knew all along it was a pump-action shotgun, then forgot I had to pump it. By way of excuses, I can only say I never fired any kind of shotgun before. Plus I wouldn't be the first stockbroker to panic in that God-awful situation. I mean, we jump out of windows because our stocks go down.

I am disappointed, though. I thought I was doing so much better. Calm under fire and all that.

Creeper urges me toward the LeSabre's trunk. A single raven squawks at us from the top of a red maple. The bird's oily black coat shines iridescent in the morning's new sunlight. The sky glows bright gold.

Creeper makes me wrap my ankles in duct tape, seal my mouth

with the same stuff, then stick my hands behind me so he can wrap my wrists. My body automatically leans forward, adjusting for the weight of my arms behind me. My first plan in these situations is always cheerful cooperation.

When he pops the Buick's trunk, I resist too late and Creeper easily pushes me inside the tight compartment. Going down, I bang my head on the trunk hinge.

Creeper lifts my feet inside and slams the lid. The compression of air pops my ears. Total darkness engulfs me, like I'm inside a steel coffin.

The engine starts. Wonder where we're going? Wonder why Creeper didn't kill me right here?

God, it's miserable being taped up like this. No scratching or nose-wiping. Noxious gases choke my lungs. So claustrophobic.

At least the LeSabre sports a decent-size trunk. All the burlap in here makes for a reasonably soft ride, too.

After an hour's drive, Creeper lifts me out of the trunk and stands me up. We're back in New Jersey at some private marina in Leonardo or Atlantic Highlands. I can see Sandy Hook directly across the water. The salty smell of the ocean invigorates my mood. Maybe we're going fishing.

He cuts the tape around my ankles and walks me out on a wooden pier. Oh, boy. The crack of dawn's a perfect time to bait fish. And those burlap bags he brought along from the trunk must be some kind of blanket to keep us warm. It's going to be cold out there on Sandy Hook Bay.

Leading me to a docked skiff, the picture suddenly becomes clear. In the bottom of the boat lie a pile of lead weights and heavy linked chain.

SIXTY-SEVEN

Cold out here on the glassy waters of Sandy Hook Bay. Downright bitter. My teeth chatter like castanets.

Creeper's massive shoulders paddled us a mile offshore in nine strokes. Faster than a two-hundred horsepower, turbocharged Evinrude. Now he's planting the oars and unfurling burlap. Gulls squawk and circle overhead. Marine vultures, each of them. Hungry and waiting.

The bullet-shaped rowboat rises and falls on low morning swells, one of the boat's two aluminum benches poking me in the ribs each lift. A thick, bluish-gray mist hovers above the ocean's calm surface, a smoky fog that smells like spoiled clams.

Despite my gloomy surroundings, the immediately preceding events, and the obvious nature of Creeper employing a chain-filled boat to transport us, I've been making a wholehearted effort not to overanalyze my future. But somehow the cold air, the chattering teeth...well, logic suggests it might be time to focus on impending death. Use the bitter cold of eternity as motivation for my absolutely finest Gift of Gab. Come on, Carr. Let him have it.

"Mmmm. Mmmm."

Oops. I forgot my lips are sealed with duct tape. Damn. This makes things more difficult, certainly. But on the plus side, when my golden tongue somehow does get me out of this impasse, Letterman, Oprah, Ripley's—they'll all want interviews. I'll have to hire a PR chick.

"Lay down on burlap," Creeper says.

I roll onto my brown, itchy shroud. Intended shroud, that is. I still have a shot. I have plans. But I wish those damn seagulls would shut up. Too much competition for Creeper's attentions.

"MMMMMM," I say.

The big man stares at me. His gray eyes are softer than I imagined, the coldness not right out front. A crooked smile forms on his razor-thin lips, reminiscent of a gash I once received from a broken beer bottle.

I wear the pink scar on my upper right arm.

"You have final words?" Creeper says. "Okay. Is big American tradition. I see plenty of movies."

He rips the tape from my mouth. Ouch. But the Great Spirit smiles on me. A chance for redemption.

"Why are you killing me, Max? Gina Farascio's the one who planned your boss's assassination, had you shot, killed your friend Jerry. Obviously you know that. You just broke her neck."

Creeper starts wrapping me in torn-up burlap bags. Burrito el Broker. "Boss, my friend both die in your friend's restaurant," he says. "Right after you leave. You are part."

This is a bum rap. "I didn't know, Max. That's why Luis sent me away. So I wouldn't be a part. Maybe Luis didn't even know. I can't imagine him allowing such a thing in his restaurant. But even if Luis knew—and I don't think he did—you can't blame him. Bluefish wanted him dead."

Creeper's monster shoulders roll forward, a shrug that slightly rocks our boat. He continues to truss me in the scratchy burlap.

Okay. It's not going to be an easy sale.

"It was Gina, Max. It was always Gina. As soon as I asked her husband to help me fend off Bluefish, Farascio's family must have decided to take Shore for themselves. It'd be easy with me in charge, Mr. Vick out of town."

You need a kicker on that one, Carr. Come on. "And they would've taken Shore if you hadn't of gotten rid of Tony and Gina for me."

Creeper's done with the burlap. Forget the burrito image. I look like a cheese-stuffed, whole-wheat Hoagie roll. Creeper's huge hands grab up a truckload of chain link. Then, one loop at a time, Creeper begins to package me in my oceangoing steel jewelry.

I'm all shiny for the ball.

"I'd be signing over Shore to the Farascio family right now if you hadn't killed her, Max. Truth is, I owe you."

205

Creeper threads two loops around my waist. The weight of the chain presses the rough burlap tight against my skin.

"Owe me?" he says.

"Definitely. You saved me—I don't know—maybe a couple of hundred grand over the next couple of years. Max might deserve a very big reward."

He throws more steel around my neck.

"Reward?" he says.

My body chills like I'm at the bottom of a grave, the cold dirt splashing against my throat and face. "Ab-so-fucking-lutely," I say. "Very big. How about I write you a check tonight for fifty thousand, plus tomorrow we write up a contract for your services? Full-time employment at Shore Securities. What do you need? Two hundred grand a year?"

Creeper removes a brass padlock from the pocket of his Dockers. His cucumber-size fingers struggle to line up the two ends of the chain. "I think no," he says.

SIXTY-EIGHT

The urge, of course, is to panic. I mean, this BS is not fooling Creeper. But—and this is a big but, a real redline rule of sales—to switch arguments now is guaranteed failure. Positive doom.

Think Niagara Falls in a tea cup.

See, with any client, you can never give up, never let them believe they know better than you. You have to maintain expert status or the whole relationship sinks. You just keep pushing benefits, asking for the order.

When he can, a big hitter like my ex-pal Walter Osgood will pick on some unique area of the client's psyche, some hollow point where the customer is particularly soft and vulnerable.

What was that story Beth told me about her time with Creeper?

"Max," I say. "Your boss is dead. So's your friend Jerry. Where the hell are you going to go? Back to the circus? Maybe they'll let you clean the cages of the lions and tigers. Those big smelly cats."

Creeper jams the lock through both ends of the chain, his jaw muscles flexing. But he hesitates...frowning before snapping that puppy shut. Oh. My. God. He's thinking about it. Creeper's actually considering my desperate and semi-ridiculous proposal.

Time to ask for the order.

"Work for me, Max. You won't be sorry. Let's go to my office right now, I'll write you that check for fifty thou. What do you say?"

Creeper stares at the still-open padlock. A passenger jet heading into Liberty-Newark cruises low in the steel blue morning sky. My heart knocks against my ribs.

Click. Creeper locks me up. The chain around me seems to double in weight, an anchor pushing me against the aluminum hull of the boat.

"Max no talk good," he says. "Cannot be stockbroker."

I work hard to keep my five o'clock-in-the-morning, full-boat Carr smile. I know it looks bad. I mean, he shut the padlock, converting my ass into a two-hundred-fifty-pound, semi-verbal fishing sinker. But the truth is, I swear I've almost got him. I know it sounds nuts, but I'm telling you. I'm close to closing him. Come on, Carr. Drive this big ugly puppy into the doghouse.

"You don't have to be a stockbroker." I say. "In fact, you don't have to say a word to anybody if you don't want to. I'll tell my employees you're a mute."

Max shakes his head. "You big liar. Your own daughter say so. Also a wimp. Elizabeth tell me about your electrical sex with own wife."

Huh? How does Beth know about that? "You mean Susan's Mobachi 3000?"

Max snorts. Then laughs. "Ha."

At least snorting is what I think his thick ugly nostrils are doing. He could be just cleaning his nose. I guess you don't pick up a lot of social etiquette wrestling bears.

I take a deep breath. Turn it around, Mr. Golden Tongue. Turn this wimp thing around.

"That should make this decision easy," I say. "I'm a trusting soul, Max. It's true. I want to get along, let everybody do what they have to do. For a tough guy like you, I'll always be an easy mark. In other words, I'm such a wimp, you can always kill me later. Anytime you feel like it. Like after you cash that fifty-thousand-dollar check."

Creeper's gaze falls to the padlock. "Is stupid idea. Max no stockbroker."

Son-of-a-bitch, this sale is still alive. "Forget stockbrokers, Max. You say nothing to anyone, except maybe 'Get the fuck out of my way.' I want you to drive my car, Max, be my bodyguard. Gina and Tony's friends might try something."

Creeper fingers the lock. His gaze climbs to the brightening Sunday morning sky. I can almost hear Creeper's square head ticking.

Slowly, he twists his face to look at me. I sense curiosity in his gray eyes.

"What kind of car Max drive?"

SIXTY-NINE

One Month Later...

"Are we going for Mexican again?"

Ryan's six-word query comes across like one long whine. Gee. I know my son doesn't like hot sauce and food overly spiced, but I thought my budding all-star shortstop enjoyed Umberto's relatively mild chicken chimichangas. He never said he didn't.

"It is my Wednesday night to pick the restaurant," I say.

Beth shakes her head. She's glaring out the passenger window of my Camry. "And that means Luis's. You haven't picked another place for us to eat on Wednesday in like, what? Three years?"

"What about that night we went to Zorro's for a masked cheeseburger?"

Beth says, "Masked cat's more like it. And the only reason we went there is because Luis's was closed after the fire."

I brake the Camry at a red light on Broad Street. A mile-long white stretch limo pulls up the light beside us, diverting my mind from repartee with Beth. Why do these limos always have blackout windows? Like if we actually saw Bruce or Mr. Bon Jovi, we might jump straight out of our cars and attack them?

Green light. I push down on the gas pedal. Thanks to the ex-wife's change of heart, I have Beth and Ryan again on Wednesday nights, plus every other weekend. When I showed Susan's attorney how well Shore was doing, what my new ownership percentage was, the man became very interested. When I showed him how I named Susan custodian of the kids' new college mutual fund accounts, well, he became almost friendly.

So did Susan, actually. Soft and gooey. She actually smiled at me tonight when I picked up the kids.

209

Go figure.

Being the one to "capture" Creeper probably helped my cause as well. Though I discouraged the idea, primarily because the perception was inaccurate, the media continually played up the sensational angle of a father using his Gift of Gab to trick a murderer, his daughter's kidnapper, into surrendering. In truth, I probably would have made Creeper my driver, as promised, if some shell-collecting beach hiker hadn't seen Creeper with Gina's shotgun, called 911 right away on his Nokia.

Those Keansburg cops swarmed us like locusts, had Creeper in handcuffs before I could explain the special conditions of his new employment.

He must have had outstanding warrants.

We hit another red light. "Tell you what, kids," I say. "As a special treat, in celebration of this modest family reunion, I'll take the two of you back to the Locust Tree Inn for steak and lobster. Bluefish and the Creeper won't be there, but maybe we'll meet some other—"

"Nooooo," Ryan and Beth say. Their combined voices vibrate the Camry's windows.

I was only kidding. I'm hitting Luis's tonight for reasons other than tequila and burritos.

"You silly," Mama Bones says. "You see those-a two pretty girls at the end of the bar?"

"Yes."

Luis's Mexican Grill is filled with Bonacelli clan members tonight—Bonacellis, and the happy crew of Shore Securities. We're having a party to celebrate Mr. Vick's return from Tuscany.

"Luis loves the girl on right," Mama Bones says. "One with dark hair and dark eyes. Her name is Angelina, too. Why you imagine Luis love my poor niece Gina? God rest her soul."

I shrug. "Luis kissed Gina at the bar the night Bluefish was killed."

She grins at me. "You jealous? Of Luis...or Gina? Ha ha ha."

"Ha ha your own bad self."

I give her the full-boat Carr grin. Don't want Mama Bones turning me into a zombie.

Mr. Vick's mother lets the twinkle in her eyes spread across her whole face. Wrinkle by wrinkle. "You such a goofball, Austin. You lucky I not ten years younger."

Ten? Hell, twenty wouldn't give her a shot. "I'm sure you were something, Mama Bones."

"You better believe."

I nod and grin like one of those bobble head dolls. I have another question on my mind. "So, before I get back to my kids over there—"

"Where?"

I nod.

"Oh, you got very beautiful children."

"Thanks. But were you the woman who called me from Clooneys that Saturday night, the person who set me up to see Franny give Gina that DVD?"

The smiles Mama Bones's face freezes. "How you figure, smarty pants?"

I knew it. "Just a hunch."

"Hunch, huh?" Mama Bones touches the wart on her chin. Wonder how she found it inside all those wrinkles. "Okay. Yeah, I call. I wanted you to see that state copper with my Gina, God rest her soul. That copper playing everybody on every side of a fence."

Mama Bones might have her villains mixed up. Blood can be thicker than truth. "But why show me? What was I going to do about it?"

"You needed to see that Anne Marie was dirty, too, that she was helping Tony's people get their paws on my son Vittorio's business."

I touch Mama Bone's shoulder. "I'm awfully sorry about Gina, Mama Bones. She was a very special person."

What I don't say: I'll never forget how Gina's bare breasts looked swinging below the stock of that pump-action. How my heart and gut felt while I watched. In my mind, Ms. Shotgun lives forever.

Mama Bones lowers her gaze. Wonder if she's up for a promotion now that her boss Bluefish is dead?

"I go back to my table now," she says. "But my Vittorio be here very, very soon. I know he is anxious to see you. But you come over to my table later, okay? I want you to meet my sister's girl, Nicky."

"Right after I talk to Vick, Mama Bones. I have some news for him."

SEVENTY

When Beth, Ryan, and I finish eating, we walk three blocks to Carvel's for ice cream. Though it's fun to show and share with my children things I liked as a kid, my job as parent isn't only to be protector and pal. Once every visit—six times a month—I exercise them like boarded horses and rein the discussion toward trails my children might not necessarily like to travel.

"So you two are studying hard in school, right?"

They both nod, Beth with somewhat less enthusiasm. Uh, oh. I used to slip in questions like this when I thought they least expected interrogation, a technique I learned watching Sipowicz. But ambush is hard these days. When I lost the element of surprise, I added the walking for ice cream.

"The grades are still good, right?" I ask. "Both of you?"

"I got all A's and B's for the year," Ryan says.

Silence from my daughter.

"Beth?" I scrunch my eyebrows when she glances at me. Never underestimate disapproval as a training tool.

"Maybe I got a C or two this time," she says.

Oh, boy. My ex-wife will have a hissy fit. Beth has been all A's and B's since kindergarten.

I lick my double-fudge chocolate on a sugar cone. "School's very important," I say. "Life is about choices. Good grades and more schooling gives you extra choices. Bad grades, no college, your career options are pretty much restaurants and hospitals. Waiting tables or changing bedpans is what our current population most craves. The Baby Boomers are eating out on their way to the nursing home."

Ryan stares straight ahead. I may have gone too far with my

explanations.

"We know the speech, Daddy," Beth says. "We need a college education to earn the Big Money."

After I drop Beth and Ryan at Susan's new house, a four-bedroom ranch two blocks from the beach, I head back to Luis's. I'm at the bar, being introduced to Luis's girlfriend, Angelina Something, when Mr. Vick parades inside the restaurant like he's one of the first astronauts coming home from the moon.

Talk about your favorite son. Takes him fifteen minutes just to hug and kiss his five sisters, Mr. Vick being passed from table to table like a bottle of ketchup. Shaking hands, slapping shoulders; laughing with the men between lip smacking the women.

With the Bonacellis, one virus gets you twenty cold sufferers.

An hour later we're finally alone. Mr. Vick says, "So business is good despite the bad publicity?"

"Oh, yeah," I say.

We're drinking margaritas at the corner table beneath Luis's wall-mounted television. The Yankees and Red Sox are playing in Boston. The whole U-shaped bar—a baseball bleacher section in disguise—cheers between us and the Bonacelli-Shore revelers. Much to the baseball fans' chagrin, Luis let Mama Bones turn up the house music for dancing. The combined roar is deafening.

Mr. Vick's coming at me slow. But he's obviously heard what I've been up to. If I know Vick, he's getting ready to jump me. Go ahead, pal. I'm ready.

"Business is real good," I say. "Like the publicity was good for us, not bad. We lost five accounts the first day, but that was pretty much the end of it. We've opened one hundred and fifty new accounts since."

Mr. Vick nods. His eyebrows pinch. Here it comes."I hear Rags is trying to sell you his seventeen percent interest in Shore," he says. "You know that's supposed to be Carmela's. What the hell do you think you're doing?"

"Sold, actually. Escrow closed today."

He frowns. "What?"

I stand up. "Come out back with me, Vick. I have something to show you."

Mr. Vick just stares at me. "Carmela's supposed to get those shares in the divorce agreement with Rags."

I show Mr. Vick my most delicious, full-boat Carr grin. "What divorce? Carmela's decided she's still in love with crazy Rags. She's down in the Caribbean with him right now, sobering him up at Eric Clapton's gold-plated rehab. Glad my money's going to such a good cause."

"You're not getting away with this crap," Vick says.

Wanna bet? I turn and hit the TV's off switch, then lean over the bar and cut the music. The sudden absence of loud noise makes everyone in the restaurant stare my way. Or maybe it's the fact I'm now standing on Luis's bar.

"Everybody come on outside," I say. "I have a special surprise for Vick and all the Bonacellis."

Lots of murmuring, but nobody wants to comment on what's tied down in the back of this giant truck I had parked in Luis's lot. Nobody but Mr. Vick, that is.

"Is this a freaking joke?" he says.

"No. In addition to Rags's shares, I also closed today on Walter's seventeen percent interest in Shore."

Mr. Vick's face turns the color of fresh snow. "What? You bought Walter's too?"

"As of noon today, I own fifty-one percent of Shore, Mr. Vick. You work for me now."

Dazed, Mr. Vick glances again at the truck's heavy load, a giant rectangular sign. The bright, red-lettered plastic will tomorrow take its place above Branchtown's busiest street. I think it might take Vick a long time to get used to our company's new name.

Carr Securities, Inc.

An early and avid reader of the Hardy Boys and Sherlock Holmes, Jack Getze wrote his first mystery stories for the high school newspaper and creative writing magazine.

He earned his first professional byline as a nineteen-year-old copyboy for the Los Angeles Herald-Examiner. He later moved to the Los Angeles Times where as a Staff Writer and Reporter he covered national economic issues for nearly a decade. Through the Los Angeles Times/Washington Post news syndicate, his news and feature stories have been published in over five-hundred newspapers and periodicals worldwide.

During a second career as a retail bond salesman and stockbroker on the New Jersey Shore he learned about financial and economic issues from the investment community's perspective.

His hobbies include reading, gardening, an occasional hike, and swimming at the beach. He lives not far from the beach in New Jersey with his wife, two of his three children, a dog, a cat, and a fish.

Printed in the United States
124798LV00001BA/253-258/P

9 781591 332398